INTERZONE

Other Books by William S. Burroughs

Edited by James Grauerholz

Viking

Interzone

William S. Burroughs

VIKING
Published by the Penguin Group
Viking Penguin Inc., 40 West 23rd Street,
New York, New York 10010, U.S.A.
Penguin Books Ltd, 27 Wrights Lane,
London W8 5TZ, England
Penguin Books Australia Ltd, Ringwood,
Victoria, Australia
Penguin Books Canada Ltd, 2801 John Street,
Markham, Ontario, Canada L3R 1B4
Penguin Books (N.Z.) Ltd, 182–190 Wairau Road,
Auckland 10, New Zealand

Penguin Books Ltd, Registered Offices:
Harmondsworth, Middlesex, England

First published in 1989 by Viking Penguin Inc.
Published simultaneously in Canada

10 9 8 7 6 5 4 3 2 1

Copyright © William S. Burroughs, 1989
All rights reserved

Passages from *Naked Lunch* used by permission of
Grove Press, a division of Wheatland Corporation.

"The Finger," "Lee's Journals,"
"An Advertising Short for TV," "Antonio the Portuguese
Mooch," "Displaced Fuzz," "Spare Ass Annie,"
and "The Dream Cops" first appeared in
Early Routines, Cadmus Editions.

"The Conspiracy" was previously published in *Kulchur*.

LIBRARY OF CONGRESS CATALOGING-IN-PUBLICATION DATA
Burroughs, William S., 1914–
Interzone.
I. Title.
PS3552.U75I5   1989   813'.54   88-40303
ISBN 0–670–81347–8

Printed in the United States of America
Set in Bodoni Book and Univers 75
Designed by Amy Hill

Contents

Introduction

William Burroughs has always presented interesting challenges to his editors. Throughout his career he has often rejected the concept of linear composition or narrative. Moreover, much of his significant work was written in times of great personal disarray and tossed off in various directions, especially to friends in correspondence. He is also one of the great recyclers in literary history, a programmatic one—in the creation of his powerful language mosaics, Burroughs will use whatever materials are at hand. The scattered circumstances of his literary efforts are reflected in the scattered provenance of much of Burroughs' archival material. In the long run, there will be plenty of work for the critics and the textual scholars of Burroughs' work to perform as they begin to unravel the tangled history of Burroughs' works: published, unpublished, and perhaps yet to be discovered.

This volume, however, may be described as a product of the medium run. This book was conceived as a response to the news in 1984 that the original manuscript of *Interzone*, the working title of the book that, in somewhat different form, was to become *Naked Lunch*, was rediscovered among Allen Ginsberg's papers at Columbia University. It was soon apparent that the *Interzone* manuscript did contain unpublished material of great value and interest. The Burroughs of the *Interzone* period was a man breaking through into unexplored literary territory.

The same is true of writings leading up to that breakthrough. Many of Burroughs' texts from the period between the completion of his novel *Queer* and the beginning of *Interzone/Naked Lunch* (roughly 1953–58) have seen publication only in fugitive ways: included, sometimes in fragmentary form, in larger works or in various collections of uncertain duration and availability. Much else of value has remained in manuscript form until this time. Until now, the reader or critic wishing to understand how the precise, laconic and deadpan writer of *Junky* and *Queer* transformed himself into the uncompromising prophet and seer of *Naked Lunch* has had to piece the puzzle together from multiple sources, with several crucial pieces missing. *Interzone* has been compiled with the intention that readers may now be able to see that transformation take place in the course of one volume.

William Burroughs was almost thirty-nine years old when he departed Mexico City for the last time, in January of 1953. He left behind him the shambles of his life until that age: a St. Louis childhood and Harvard education, followed by a miscellany of odd jobs in Chicago and New York. In 1944 he had first become addicted to heroin; in that same year he met Allen Ginsberg at Columbia. These two circumstances would have a profound effect on his development as a writer.

As Burroughs' legal difficulties from his addiction mounted, he was obliged to move on from New York: to East Texas, New Orleans, and finally Mexico City, while Ginsberg and Jack Kerouac remained in New York, giving rise to an ample correspondence, which in turn led directly to Burroughs' discovery of his writing talents. Ginsberg enjoyed the intelligence and humor of Burroughs' letters from the far-flung precincts of Louisiana and Mexico, and he continually encouraged Burroughs to consider himself a writer.

A forged-prescription arrest had precipitated the departure from New York, in 1946; in New Orleans a 1949 marijuana arrest had put him through the rigors of heroin withdrawal in a jail cell; and although at first blush he found the liberal mores of Mexico much to his liking, in time the abuse of drugs and alcohol led to the careless, accidental death of his wife, Joan Vollmer, on September 6, 1951. A drunken pistol game of William Tell in an apartment above the Bounty Bar ended in tragedy for both.

In the spring of 1950, after about six months in Mexico City, Burroughs had begun writing a first-person account of his experiences in the junk world, which he entitled *Junk*. Ginsberg's friend Carl Solomon had interested his uncle in publishing such an account as an Ace Books paperback, and a contract was signed in July 1952. The book appeared as *Junkie: Confessions of an Unredeemed Drug Addict* a year later. Not included in this text was the second part of the original book, entitled *Queer*, which was begun in the spring of 1951. (*Junkie* was re-edited, with censored passages restored, and republished as *Junky* by Viking Penguin in 1977; *Queer* was finally published by Viking in 1985.)

As *Queer* relates, Burroughs was infatuated with a young American boy called Allerton and took him along on a trip to Ecuador in a fruitless search for *yagé*, a reputedly telepathic drug. He returned to Mexico City only days before the fatal incident. During the course of the novel, the protagonist, Lee, develops and elaborates an absurdist form of soliloquy known as the "routine," in his constant attempts to capture and hold Allerton's attention under increasingly difficult circumstances. This "Tom Sawyer handstand meant to impress the work's *blaue Blume*, Eugene Allerton," as Alan Ansen* describes it, takes on a life of its own, even as Allerton is drifting away from Lee.

As Burroughs recounts in "Lee's Journals" (page 63), he was often "possessed by a wild routine. . . . These routines will reduce me to a cinder." Such intensity naturally sought a human outlet, and as Allerton became emotionally distanced, and with Joan gone, Burroughs' friendship with Allen Ginsberg took on greater significance. After giving up on Allerton and Mexico City in late 1952, he made a visit to his parents' home in Palm Beach, Florida, and from there departed for Panama and the headwaters of the Río Putumayo in Colombia. Not two weeks after reaching Panama City, he wrote the first of what would be many "letters from the road" to Ginsberg, retailing his travels and adventures in a hilarious mixture of amorous anecdotes and anthropological essays.

Burroughs returned to the U.S. in August 1953, and after a month in Palm Beach, he returned to New York for the first time in six years. *Junkie* had now been published, and although it was hardly considered a literary event at the time, this encouraged him to go on with his writing. He stayed on East Seventh Street with Ginsberg, whose constant interest and warm responses to the stream of "*yagé* letters" had endeared him to Burroughs, far beyond anything he had felt for Ginsberg before. They worked together on a revised transcription of Burroughs' letters from the *yagé* trip, but Burroughs' dream of finding in Ginsberg the "perfectly sponta-

* Alan Ansen, *William Burroughs* (Sudbury, Mass.: Water Row Press, 1986).

neous, perfectly responsive companion" (Ansen, *ibid.*) was frustrated by Allen's lack of interest in a sexual relationship.

In early 1954 Burroughs sailed for Rome, Athens and eventually Tangier. He continued to woo Ginsberg during the middle fifties, entirely by correspondence, except for a memorable visit that Ginsberg and his new lover, Peter Orlovsky, made to Tangier in 1957. In his letters from the time of the visit, Ginsberg writes that he scarcely recognized "the new Bill Burroughs." By then Burroughs had almost completed the transition from suitor-correspondent to literary creator, which resulted in a profusion of manuscripts that he referred to in toto as *Interzone*. In these four crucial years, 1954–57, Burroughs had been transformed into a writer.

As he had done with *Junky* and the handful of more or less finished stories that Burroughs sent from Tangier to him in New York, Ginsberg assisted in the editing of the early drafts of *Interzone*. While visiting in 1957, he retyped portions of the raw manuscripts, as did Jack Kerouac and Alan Ansen, and they each proposed different chapter sequences. The best account of their attitudes toward the work at that time can be gleaned from Alan Ansen's pioneering and perceptive essay in *Big Table* in 1959, "Anyone Who Can Pick Up a Frying Pan Owns Death," collected in his 1986 Water Row Press booklet.

In April 1958, on Ginsberg's referral, Burroughs submitted a draft of *Interzone* to Lawrence Ferlinghetti's City Lights Books (by now the publishers of Ginsberg's *Howl*), but it was not accepted. Maurice Girodias of the Olympia Press in Paris also turned down the book. Ginsberg sent eighty pages of Burroughs' work to Irving Rosenthal, editor of the *Chicago Review*, but when University of Chicago authorities objected, Rosenthal published an issue privately as *Big Table, No. 1* in the spring of 1959. Included were ten episodes from *Interzone*, which was by then called *Naked Lunch*, at Kerouac's suggestion. Within a few months, Girodias had published the novel in France. The rest is literary history.

What remains of these early writings, between the period of composition of *Junky* and *Queer* and the publication of *Naked Lunch*? The letters from South America during 1953 were finally edited, with letters added from Ginsberg's own 1960 trip to Peru in search of *yagé*, and responses from Burroughs, and this book was published as *The Yagé Letters* by City Lights in 1963. A short collection of stories, journals and letter fragments was edited for publication in 1982 by Jeffrey Miller's Cadmus Editions in Santa Barbara, in a small edition now out of print, under the title *Early Routines*. A large surviving group of letters to Ginsberg was also published in 1982, under the eponymous title *Letters to Allen Ginsberg, 1953–1957*, by Full Court Press; this volume, also now out of print, is a valuable companion to the present *Interzone*.

Many of these 1950s writings are fragmentary in nature; in many cases, pages that began as letters to Ginsberg were not sent but condensed and retyped together with other material; the letters that *were* sent included long patches of work in progress. Therefore the lines between "letters," "journals" and "writings" are blurred, at least as regards the manuscript material that remains available from the period. And Burroughs' papers have had a harrowing voyage to the hands of today's scholars: what exists from the period (mostly at Columbia University, Arizona State University and the Humanities Research Center of the University of Texas at Austin, as well as the author's own collection) is jumbled and incomplete, and many other manuscripts remain in uncooperative private hands at this writing. So what is included in this volume has been determined, in part, and fittingly enough, by random factors.

One of the hallmarks of Burroughs' style is the reappearance of many phrases and images throughout his work. This is partly the result of Burroughs' multifarious memory, partly due to the chaos of his manuscript drafts, and partly inherent in the nature of the "cut-up" technique. This "repetition," or self-appropriation, may even at times be unintentional, but overall it unites the whole of

Burroughs' work and lends a kaleidoscopic quality to the writing—and what is a kaleidoscope but a device to reassemble endlessly the same particles? As if anticipating modern atomic physics, his world model is that of an indeterminate universe of endless permutation and recombination. Finding the conventional novel form inadequate to this task, he deconstructs and ransacks it, so that his form is as reflective of twentieth-century life as his content is predictive of it.

"Twilight's Last Gleamings" is often cited as Burroughs' first attempt at writing; it was written in Cambridge, Massachusetts, in 1938, with the collaboration of his childhood friend Kells Elvins. The thirteen-page manuscript at Arizona does not appear to be the original but a reconstruction from memory at some later point, when Burroughs was using a typewriter with the Spanish inverted exclamation point, hence probably in Tangier. The author has written that the piece was inspired by the sinking of a ship, the *Morro Castle*, in 1935, and this rollicking, exploding fantasy pointed the way toward his eventual literary destination. Much shorter versions of it have appeared throughout his writings, most notably in *Nova Express* (Grove, 1964); this is the fullest version yet published.

"The Finger" is an account of how Burroughs deliberately cut off the last joint of his left little finger, in New York during 1939, partly in an attempt to impress Jack Anderson, a young man with whom he was preoccupied. This chilling episode gives a rare glimpse of Burroughs' emotional state at that time. In a letter to Ginsberg from Tangier, apparently written in 1954, he mentions having sent the story to Allen to see if it could be sold for publication; so it was probably written soon after his arrival in Tangier.

"Driving Lesson" is a quasi-autobiographical account of an incident from 1940, during Jack Anderson's visit to Burroughs in

St. Louis. It seems to have been written during Burroughs' Mexico stay but was in any case rewritten and sent to Ginsberg sometime in 1954. In a letter of August 18, 1954, Burroughs wrote: "As regards that story, you might try placing it, I don't know just where"; and again, August 26: "I rewrote the story about the car wreck with Jack A." In *The Wild Boys* (Grove, 1971) and *Port of Saints* (Am Here, 1974; Blue Wind, 1980), the car has become a Duesenberg, and Jack is "the new boy, John Hamlin," "a mysterious figure from a parallel dimension"; the crash itself takes on the magical power of time travel.

"The Junky's Christmas" dates from Mexico or early Tangier days, and is set in New York in the 1940s. Danny the Car Wiper is a young junky trying desperately to score on Christmas Day. His experiences are written in a straightforward third-person narrative style, somewhat reminiscent of Truman Capote's. This sentimental story was the basis of a later, and much different, story: "The Priest, They Called Him," published in the London *Weekend Telegraph* in 1967 and collected in *Exterminator!* (Viking, 1973). Burroughs has written several "Christmas stories" over the years, but never again in this style.

"Lee and the Boys" appears to have been written in the Tangier period. The untitled story begins in manuscript on a page with paragraphs also found in an April 1954 letter to Ginsberg. Although it has an indeterminate ending, it is worth reproducing here for its remarkably straightforward and detailed self-portrait of Burroughs' daily life in Tangier at that time. We see him scoring his drugs, shooting up and sitting down to work on a "letter to Ginsberg," and then receiving his boyfriend KiKi for an evening's diversion. His emotions about the boys of Tangier are heartbreakingly felt, and his bravado has a tremulous edge.

"In the Café Central," also from this time, is a very funny sketch of the social scene in the Socco Chico, written without much of Burroughs' trademark exaggeration. The claustrophobia of Tangier's small-town feel, at least among the expatriate queer set, comes across vividly.

"Dream of the Penal Colony" is labeled in manuscript "Fall of 1953," which suggests it was written in New York at the beginning of Burroughs' stay with Ginsberg. Its point of departure is the first paragraph of the passage in *Queer* where Lee and Allerton are staying in a chilly hotel room in Quito, Ecuador: "That night Lee dreamed he was in a penal colony. All around were high, bare mountains. . . . He tightened the belt of his leather jacket and felt the chill of final despair." In the novel, Lee gets up and crawls into Allerton's bed, shaking with cold and junk sickness. The parallel suggested is between Allerton and Ginsberg, objects of Burroughs' affection and desire, and if this fragment was actually not written until after work on *Queer* stopped, in late 1952, the compositional intention toward Ginsberg is even clearer. But the boy in the story is modeled on Allerton, and the author paints a harsh picture of his own manipulative, changing moods and importuning routines.

"International Zone" was written in a deliberate attempt to achieve a magazine sale, via Ginsberg. The name of the piece refers, of course, to the quadripartite administration of Tangier, divided between the U.S., French, Spanish and English sectors. On January 12, 1955, Burroughs wrote to Ginsberg: "When I don't have inspiration for the novel [*Interzone*, then in progress], I busy myself with hack work. I am writing an article on Tangier. Perhaps *New Yorker*: 'Letter from Tangier.' " Again, on January 21: "I wrote an article on Tangier but it depresses me to see it even. It is so flatly an article like anybody could have written." On this point the author was mistaken; the language and style are distinctively his own. Here, between sociological information and analysis, are several incisive portraits of the habitués of the Socco Chico, and a snapshot of Burroughs' own image of himself on that set.

"International Zone" was apparently sent to Ginsberg in the

summer of 1955, perhaps nine months after it was first composed. In the original manuscript there is a postscript (not included in the piece as presented here), which exemplifies a typically Burroughsian shift of viewpoint on a new locale:

"Since I wrote this article, conditions in Tangier have changed. There is a strong feeling of tension and hostility. Children shout insults as you walk by. The streets are no longer safe. A Canadian acquaintance of mine, coming home at 3 A.M., was stabbed in the back. . . . The Nationalists have already demanded the integration of Tangier into an independent Morocco. They may resort to terrorism if the occupying powers refuse to relinquish the International Zone. . . . Business has hit a new low. The tourist trade is falling off. Many of the residents are talking about leaving." This shift echoes the transformation of Mexico City, from being "one of the few places left where a man can really live like a Prince," in Burroughs' 1949 letters to Ginsberg, to "this cold ass town," in a letter from late 1952, again to Ginsberg: "I am so fed up with these chiseling bastards I don't ever want to see Mexico again."

In late 1954, when "International Zone" was composed, Burroughs was changing his view of Tangier as a superlatively liberal culture where boys and drugs were concerned, to a vision of the City as a great world crossroads for losers and lamsters, an "interzone" between failed and abandoned old lives (like Burroughs' own) and the dream of a new life ahead—the sort of "waiting room" that is a recurrent image in Burroughs' fiction. In the article, he writes that "Tangier is a vast penal colony," which again recalls the dream he had in Quito in 1951. Especially interesting is Burroughs' self-portrait as "Brinton, who writes unpublishably obscene novels and exists on a small income. He undoubtedly has talent, but his work is hopelessly unsalable."

This same passage is echoed in the first pages of "Lee's Journals," which were assembled from sections of letters to Ginsberg and pages written in Burroughs' attempt to find his own voice and to record his experiences in Tangier. Also included here are several short untitled fictional and autobiographical sketches, many written during his series of heroin "cures" at Benchimal Hospital. The fag scene of Tangier is bitingly depicted, and it is interesting to observe that Burroughs' first encounters with the late Brion Gysin ("Algren") were ambivalent, giving no hint of the almost symbiotic friendship the two men would later evolve.

The sketch (in "Lee's Journals") of "Martin" revisiting the Römanischer Baden in postwar Vienna surely draws on Burroughs' own experiences in that city in 1937. And "Mark Bradford," the playwright visiting Tangier who snubs Lee, may well be Tennessee Williams, with whom Burroughs did not become friends until the 1970s. Similarly, at his 1954 meeting with Paul Bowles, the latter "evinced no cordiality," but within two years not only was their friendship forged but Bowles had also brought Burroughs back together with Brion Gysin.

Increasingly, the journals record Burroughs' attempts to define himself as a writer, and the frantic routines continue to pour out of him. His extended sketch of Antonio, the Portuguese mooch mentioned in "International Zone," is hilarious and ghastly. The vision of Antonio's mother's kidney-dialysis machine being unhooked leads to a wise-guy cops routine about the "displaced fuzz" paying a disconnection visit. There follows an account of a bust by "dream cops," which is the forerunner of the "Hauser and O'Brien" section of *Naked Lunch*: two imaginary cops burst in on "the Agent" and demand to inspect first his arm, then his penis. After a surreal dialogue, they depart, but one of them laughs and leaves behind a gold filling, which the Agent finds next morning, calling the irreality of the dream into question.

Some filling in is necessary for the next section, "The Conspiracy," to make narrative sense. In the "Hauser and O'Brien" episode, the Agent or "Lee" shoots the two cops dead and escapes from the hotel. He finds his pusher, Nick, and explains that he is leaving town and must stock up on junk. Nick makes small talk about the connection's frequent delays, and then shrugs: "What can I say to him? He knows I'll wait." At this point "The Conspiracy" picks up: "Yes, they know we'll wait," and Lee muses over the identity of the stoolie who has fingered him. The pages that follow were taken from the original 1958 *Interzone* manuscript.

"Iron Wrack Dream," so named by Ginsberg, records a vision of "the City" as "a vast network of levels . . . connected by gangways and cars that run on wires and single tracks." This futuristic dream was to be seminal to Burroughs' image of the City in *Interzone*. The nightclubs that are "built on perilous balconies a thousand feet over the rubbish and rusty metal of the City" are reminiscent of Lee's experiences in the "Mexico City Return" section of *Queer*: "I walked around with my camera and saw a wood and corrugated-iron shack on a limestone cliff in Old Panama, like a penthouse." They also call to mind the collapsing Mexican balconies of "Tío Mate Smiles" in *The Wild Boys*. Here we can see how Burroughs refines and poetically cross-associates his observations and dream images.

Incomplete fragments of unpublished letters to Ginsberg around 1955, or retyped versions of them, are found in the Arizona State collection and fittingly conclude "Lee's Journals," since they furnish an explicit statement of the literary direction Burroughs was moving in. As he wrote to Ginsberg on October 21, 1955: "The selection chapters [of *Interzone*] form a sort of mosaic, with the cryptic significance of juxtaposition, like objects abandoned in a hotel drawer, a form of still life." It is clear from these early thematic propositions that Burroughs' first encounter in 1959 with the "cut-up" method of writing, as developed by Brion Gysin from the Dada movement's existing aleatory and collage techniques, would exert an inescapable attraction for him and revolutionize his work.

The original *Interzone* manuscript is located in the Ginsberg

Deposit at Butler Library, Columbia University, and consists of 175 pages, comprising twelve sections: "WORD"; "Panorama (Andrew Kief and the K.Y. Scandal)"; "Voices"; "County Clerk"; "Interzone University"; "Islam, Inc."; "Hassan's Rumpus Room"; "Benway"; "A.J.'s Annual Ball"; "Hospital" (including the "detective story" later divided into "Hauser and O'Brien" and "The Conspiracy"); "The Technical Psychiatry Conference"; and "The Market." This first sequence was decided upon with the help of Ginsberg and Ansen in Paris, in early 1958.

In the course of assembling the final *Naked Lunch* manuscript, the majority of these pages were used—but the longest and most unusual section, "WORD," was the source of only a few short lines and paragraphs, which were sprinkled mostly into the novel's final chapter, "An Atrophied Preface . . . Wouldn't You?" Wherever possible, these passages have been deleted from the otherwise intact "WORD" section, but the acute reader will find a handful of them retained, for the sake of the sense of surrounding lines. And a few short sections that remained unused from "Voices," "Interzone University," "Benway" and "A.J.'s Annual Ball" have been inserted at an appropriate place toward the end of "WORD," so that the text may end as it was originally written.

This manuscript lay forgotten for twenty-five years, until Bill Morgan, who was cataloging Allen Ginsberg's Columbia deposit, came across it in 1984. At Ginsberg's suggestion, a copy was sent to Burroughs in Kansas, where he was able to oversee the editing of the thematically and historically linked materials gathered together in this volume, which represents the first publication of "WORD," essentially in its entirety. This chapter was apparently typed by Kerouac, and in certain instances words that were clearly misread have been changed, but it is otherwise faithful to the 1958 text.

What is the significance of "WORD" to Burroughs' career as a writer? It shows the complete transformation of the straightforward style of the two early novels into a manic, surreal, willfully disgusting and violently purgative regurgitation of seemingly random images. "WORD" is a text written at the white heat of Burroughs' first command of this later style. Although it is the direct precursor of *Naked Lunch*, very little of this text was used in that novel, and as far as can be readily determined, none of it was utilized in the composition of his next three books: *The Soft Machine, The Ticket That Exploded* and *Nova Express* (Olympia Press, 1961, 1962 and 1964). Ansen described it as: "WORD, in which the author, all masks thrown aside, delivers a long tirade, a blend of confession, routine and fantasy, ending in 'a vast Moslem muttering.' "

In his letters to Ginsberg throughout 1955–57, Burroughs wrote often of his progress with the writing of *Interzone*. December 20, 1956: "I will send along about 100 pages of *Interzone*, it is coming so fast I can hardly get it down, and shakes me like a great black wind through the bones." January 23, 1957: "*Interzone* is coming like dictation, I can't keep up with it. I will send along what is done so far. Read in any order. It makes no difference." There exist many other references in these letters; clearly, he was conscious of a climactic moment in his life, a turning point past which he would never be the same. But curiously, the tone and style of "WORD" are unique in Burroughs' work; he never returned to the same kind of profane, first-person sibylline word salad, although it marked the breakthrough into his own characteristic voice.

This book is meant to portray the development of Burroughs' mature writing style, and to present a selection of vintage Burroughs from the mid-1950s—a kind of writing he can no more repeat than he can once again be forty-four years old in Tangier. The willfully outrageous tone of voice represents the exorcism of his four decades of oppressive sexual and social conditioning, and his closely-observed experience of mankind's inexhaustible ugliness and ignorance. Only by dispensing with any concept of "bad taste" or self-repression could he liberate his writing instrument to explore the landscapes of Earth and Space in his work written over the following thirty years. Reading *Interzone*, you are present at the beginning.

—*James Grauerholz*

I. STORIES

TWILIGHT'S LAST GLEAMINGS

PLEASE IMAGINE AN EXPLOSION ON A SHIP

A paretic named Perkins sat askew on his broken wheelchair. He arranged his lips.

"You pithyathed thon of a bidth!" he shouted.

Barbara Cannon, a second-class passenger, lay naked in a first-class bridal suite with Stewart Lindy Adams. Lindy got out of bed and walked over to a window and looked out.

"Put on your clothes, honey," he said. "There's been an accident."

A first-class passenger named Mrs. Norris was thrown out of bed by the explosion. She lay there shrieking until her maid came and helped her up.

"Bring me my wig and my kimono," she told the maid. "I'm going to see the captain."

Dr. Benway, ship's doctor, drunkenly added two inches to a four-inch incision with one stroke of his scalpel.

"There was a little scar, Doctor," said the nurse, who was peering over his shoulder. "Perhaps the appendix is already out."

"The appendix *out!*" the doctor shouted. "*I'm* taking the appendix out! What do you think I'm doing here?"

"Perhaps the appendix is on the left side," said the nurse. "That happens sometimes, you know."

"Can't you be quiet?" said the doctor. "I'm coming to that!" He threw back his elbows in a movement of exasperation. "Stop breathing down my neck!" he yelled. He thrust a red fist at her. "And get me another scalpel. This one has no edge to it."

He lifted the abdominal wall and searched along the incision. "I know where an appendix is. I studied appendectomy in 1904 at Harvard."

The floor tilted from the force of the explosion. The doctor reeled back and hit the wall.

"Sew her up!" he said, peeling off his gloves. "I can't be expected to work under such conditions!"

At a table in the bar sat Christopher Hitch, a rich liberal; Colonel Merrick, retired; Billy Hines of Newport; and Joe Bane, writer.

"In all my experience as a traveler," the Colonel was saying, "I have never encountered such service."

Billy Hines twisted his glass, watching the ice cubes. "Frightful service," he said, his face contorted by a suppressed yawn.

"Do you think the captain controls this ship?" said the Colonel, fixing Christopher Hitch with a bloodshot blue eye. "Unions!" shouted the Colonel. "Unions control this ship!"

Hitch gave out with a laugh that was supposed to be placating but ended up oily. "Things aren't so bad, really," he said, patting at the Colonel's arm. He didn't land the pat, because the Colonel drew his arm out of reach. "Things will adjust themselves."

Joe Bane looked up from his drink of straight rye. "It's like I say, Colonel," he said. "A man—"

The table left the floor and the glasses crashed. Billy Hines remained seated, looking blankly at the spot where his glass had been. Christopher Hitch rose uncertainly. Joe Bane jumped up and ran away.

"By God!" said the Colonel. "I'm not surprised!"

Also at a table in the bar sat Philip Bradshinkel, investment banker; his wife, Joan Bradshinkel; Branch Morton, a St. Louis politician; and Morton's wife, Mary Morton. The explosion knocked their table over.

Joan raised her eyebrows in an expression of sour annoyance. She looked at her husband and sighed.

"I'm sorry this happened, dear," said her husband. "Whatever it is, I mean."

Mary Morton said, "Well, I declare!"

Branch Morton stood up, pushing back his chair with a large red hand. "Wait here," he said. "I'll find out."

—

Mrs. Norris pushed through a crowd on C Deck. She rang the elevator bell and waited. She rang again and waited. After five minutes she walked up to A Deck.

The Negro orchestra, high on marijuana, remained seated after the explosion. Branch Morton walked over to the orchestra leader.

"Play 'The Star-Spangled Banner,' " he ordered.

The orchestra leader looked at him.

"What you say?" he asked.

"You black baboon, play 'The Star-Spangled Banner' on your horn!"

"Contract don't say nothing 'bout no Star-Spangled Banner," said a thin Negro in spectacles.

"This old boat am swinging on down!" someone in the orchestra yelled, and the musicians jumped down off the platform and scattered among the passengers.

Branch Morton walked over to a jukebox in a corner of the saloon. He saw "The Star-Spangled Banner" by Fats Waller. He put in a handful of quarters. The machine clicked and buzzed and began to play:

"OH SAY CAN YOU? YES YES"

Joe Bane fell against the door of his stateroom and plunged in. He threw himself on the bed and drew his knees up to his chin. He began to sob.

His wife sat on the bed and talked to him in a gentle hypnotic voice. "You can't stay here, Joey. This bed is going underwater. You can't stay here."

Gradually the sobbing stopped and Bane sat up. She helped him put on a life belt. "Come along," she said.

"Nobody goes on this lifeboat but the crew," said the sailor.

"Oh, I understand," said Bradshinkel, pulling out a wad of bills. The sailor snatched the money.

"I thought so," said Bradshinkel. He took his wife by the arm and started to help her into the lifeboat.

"Get that old meat outa here!" screamed the sailor.

"But you made a bargain! You took my money!"

"Oh for Chrissakes," said the sailor. "I just took your dough so it wouldn't get wet!"

"But my wife is a woman!"

Suddenly the sailor became very gentle.

"All my life," he said, "all my life I been a sucker for a classy dame. I seen 'em in the Sunday papers laying on the beach. Soft messy tits. They just lay there and smile dirty. Jesus they heat my pants!"

Bradshinkel nudged his wife. "Smile at him." He winked at the sailor. "What do you say?"

"Naw," said the sailor, "I ain't got time to lay her now."

"Later," said Bradshinkel.

"Later's no good. Besides she's special built for you. She can't give me no kids and she drinks alla time. Like I say, I just seen her in the Sunday papers and wanted her like a dog wants rotten meat."

"Let me talk to this man," said Branch Morton. He worked his fingers over the fleshy shoulder of his wife and pulled her under his armpit.

"This little woman is a mother," he said. The sailor blew his nose on the deck. Morton grabbed the sailor by the biceps.

"In Clayton, Missouri, seven kids whisper her name through their thumbs before they go to sleep."

The sailor pulled his arm free. Morton dropped both hands to his sides, palms facing forward.

"As man to man," he was pleading. "As man to man."

"Yes, honey face," he said, and followed her out th

"AND THE HOME OF THE BRAVE"

Mrs. Norris found the door to the captain's cabin
pushed it open and stepped in, knocking on the open do
thin, red-haired man with horn-rimmed glasses was si
desk littered with maps. He glanced up without speakin

"Oh Captain, is the ship sinking? Someone set off a bc
said. I'm Mrs. Norris—you know, Mr. Norris, shipping
Oh the ship *is* sinking! I know, or you'd say something.
you will take care of us? My maid and me?" She put ou
to touch the captain's arm. The ship listed suddenly, thro
heavily against the desk. Her wig slipped.

The captain stood up. He snatched the wig off her h
put it on.

"Give me that kimono!" he ordered.

Mrs. Norris screamed. She started for the door. The
took three long, springy strides and blocked her way. Mrs
rushed for a window, screaming. The captain took a revol
his side pocket. He aimed at her bald pate outlined in the
and fired.

"You Goddamned old fool," he said. "Give me that kir

Philip Bradshinkel walked up to a sailor with his affable

"Room for the ladies on this one?" he asked, indic
lifeboat.

The sailor looked at him sourly.

"No!" said the sailor. He turned away and went on work
the launching davit.

"Now wait a minute," said Bradshinkel. "You can't mea
Women and children first, you know."

Two Negro musicians, their eyes gleaming, came up behind the two wives. One took Mrs. Morton by the arm, the other took Mrs. Bradshinkel.

"Can us have dis dance witchu?"

"THAT OUR FLAG WAS STILL THERE"

Captain Kramer, wearing Mrs. Norris' kimono and wig, his face heavily smeared with cold cream, and carrying a small suitcase, walked down to C Deck, the kimono billowing out behind him. He opened the side door to the purser's office with a pass key. A thin-shouldered man in a purser's uniform was stuffing currency and jewels into a suitcase in front of an open safe.

The captain's revolver swung free of his brassiere and he fired twice.

"SO GALLANTLY STREAMING"

Finch, the radio operator, washed down bicarbonate of soda and belched into his hand. He put the glass down and went on tapping out S.O.S.

"S.O.S. . . . S.S. *America* . . . S.O.S. . . . off Jersey coast . . . S.O.S. . . . son-of-a-bitching set . . . S.O.S. . . . might smell us . . . S.O.S. . . . son-of-a-bitching crew . . . S.O.S. . . . *Comrade* Finch . . . comrade in a pig's ass . . . S.O.S. . . . Goddamned captain's a brown artist . . . S.O.S. . . . S.S. *America* . . . S.O.S. . . . S.S. Crapbox . . ."

Lifting his kimono with his left hand, the captain stepped in behind the radio operator. He fired one shot into the back of Finch's head. He shoved the small body aside and smashed the radio with a chair.

"O'ER THE RAMPARTS WE WATCH"

Dr. Benway, carrying his satchel, pushed through the passengers crowded around Lifeboat No. 1.

"Are you all all right?" he shouted, seating himself among the women. "I'm the doctor."

"BY THE ROCKETS' RED GLARE"

When the captain reached Lifeboat No. 1 there were two seats left. Some of the passengers were blocking each other as they tried to force their way in, others were pushing forward a wife, a mother, or a child. The captain shoved them all out of his way, leapt into the boat and sat down. A boy pushed through the crowd in the captain's wake.

"Please," he said. "I'm only thirteen."

"Yes yes," said the captain, "you can sit by me."

The boat started jerkily toward the water, lowered by four male passengers. A woman handed her baby to the captain.

"Take care of my baby, for God's sake!"

Joe Bane landed in the boat and slithered noisily under a thwart. Dr. Benway cast off the ropes. The doctor and the boy started to row. The captain looked back at the ship.

"OH SAY CAN YOU SEE"

A third-year divinity student named Titman heard Perkins in his stateroom, yelling for his attendant. He opened the door and looked in.

"What do you want, thicken thit?" said Perkins.

"I want to help you," said Titman.

"Thtick it up and thwitht it!" said Perkins.

"Easy does it," said Titman, walking over toward the broken wheelchair. "Everything is going to be okey-dokey."

"Thneaked off!" Perkins put a hand on one hip and jerked the elbow forward in a grotesque indication of dancing. "Danthing with floothies!"

"We'll find him," said Titman, lifting Perkins out of the wheelchair. He carried the withered body in his arms like a child. As Titman walked out of the stateroom, Perkins snatched up a butcher knife used by his attendant to make sandwiches.

"Danthing with floothies!"

"BY THE DAWN'S EARLY LIGHT"

A crowd of passengers was fighting around Lifeboat No. 7. It was the last boat that could be launched. They were using bottles, broken deck chairs and fire axes. Titman, carrying Perkins in his arms, made his way through the fighting unnoticed. He placed Perkins in a seat at the stern.

"There you are," said Titman. "All set."

Perkins said nothing. He sat there, chin drawn back, eyes shining, the butcher knife clutched rigidly in one hand.

A hysterical crowd from second class began pushing from behind. A big-faced shoe clerk with long yellow teeth grabbed Mrs. Bane and shoved her forward. "Ladies first!" he yelled.

A wedge of men formed behind him and pushed. A shot sounded and Mrs. Bane fell forward, hitting the lifeboat. The wedge broke, rolling and scrambling. A man in an ROTC uniform with a .45 automatic in his hand stood by the lifeboat. He covered the sailor at the launching davit.

"Let this thing down!" he ordered.

As the lifeboat slid down toward the water, a cry went up from the passengers on deck. Some of them jumped into the water, others were pushed by the people behind.

"Let 'er go, God damn it, let 'er go!" yelled Perkins.

"Throw him out!"

A hand rose out of the water and closed on the side of the boat. Springlike, Perkins brought the knife down. The fingers fell into the boat and the bloody stump of hand slipped back into the water.

The man with the gun was standing in the stern. "Get going!" he ordered. The sailors pulled hard on the oars.

Perkins worked feverishly, chopping on all sides. "Bathtardth, thonthabitheth!" The swimmers screamed and fell away from the boat.

"That a boy."

"Don't let 'em swamp us."

"Atta boy, Comrade."

"Bathtardth, thonthabitheth! Bathtardth, thonthabitheth!"

"OH SAY DO DAT STAR-SPANGLED BANNER YET WAVE"

The Evening News

Barbara Cannon showed your reporter her souvenirs of the disaster: a life belt autographed by the crew, and a severed human finger.

"I don't know," said Miss Cannon. "I feel sorta bad about this old finger."

"O'ER THE LAND OF THE FREE"

THE FINGER

Lee walked slowly up Sixth Avenue from 42nd Street, looking in pawnshop windows.

"I must do it," he repeated to himself.

Here it was. A cutlery store. He stood there shivering, with the collar of his shabby chesterfield turned up. One button had fallen off the front of his overcoat, and the loose threads twisted in a cold wind. He moved slowly around the shopwindow and into the entrance, looking at knives and scissors and pocket microscopes and air pistols and take-down tool kits with the tools snapping or screwing into a metal handle, the whole kit folding into a small leather packet. Lee remembered getting one of these kits for Christmas when he was a child.

Finally he saw what he was looking for: poultry shears like the ones his father used to cut through the joints when he carved the turkey at Grandmother's Thanksgiving dinners. There they were, glittering and stainless, one blade smooth and sharp, the other with teeth like a saw to hold the meat in place for cutting.

Lee went in and asked to see the shears. He opened and closed the blades, tested the edge with his thumb.

"That's stainless steel, sir. Never rusts or tarnishes."

"How much?"

"Two dollars and seventy-nine cents plus tax."

"Okay."

The clerk wrapped the shears in brown paper and taped the package neatly. It seemed to Lee that the crackling paper made a deafening noise in the empty store. He paid with his last five dollars, and walked out with the shears heavy in his overcoat pocket.

He walked up Sixth Avenue, repeating: "I must do it. I've got to do it now that I've bought the shears." He saw a sign: *Hotel Aristo*.

There was no lobby. He walked up a flight of stairs. An old man, dingy and indistinct like a faded photograph, was standing behind a desk. Lee registered, paid one dollar in advance, and picked up a key with a heavy bronze tag.

His room opened onto a dark shaft. He turned on the light. Black stained furniture, a double bed with a thin mattress and sagging springs. Lee unwrapped the shears and held them in his hand. He put the shears down on the dresser in front of an oval mirror that turned on a pivot.

Lee walked around the room. He picked up the shears again and placed the end joint of his left little finger against the saw teeth, lower blade exactly at the knuckle. Slowly he lowered the cutting blade until it rested against the flesh of his finger. He looked in the mirror, composing his face into the supercilious mask of an eighteenth-century dandy. He took a deep breath, pressed the handle quick and hard. He felt no pain. The finger joint fell on the dresser. Lee turned his hand over and looked at the stub. Blood spurted up and hit him in the face. He felt a sudden deep pity for the finger joint that lay there on the dresser, a few drops of blood gathering around the white bone. Tears came to his eyes.

"It didn't do anything," he said in a broken child's voice. He adjusted his face again, cleaned the blood off it with a towel, and bandaged his finger crudely, adding more gauze as the blood soaked through. In a few minutes the bleeding had stopped. Lee picked up the finger joint and put it in his vest pocket. He walked out of the hotel, tossing his key on the desk.

"I've done it," he said to himself. Waves of euphoria swept through him as he walked down the street. He stopped in a bar and ordered a double brandy, meeting all eyes with a level, friendly stare. Goodwill flowed out of him for everyone he saw, for the whole world. A lifetime of defensive hostility had fallen from him.

Half an hour later he was sitting with his analyst on a park bench in Central Park. The analyst was trying to persuade him to go to Bellevue, and had suggested they "go outside to talk it over."

"Really, Bill, you're doing yourself a great disservice. When you realize what you've done you'll need psychiatric care. Your ego will be overwhelmed."

"All I need is to have this finger sewed up. I've got a date tonight."

"Really, Bill, I don't see how I can continue as your psychiatrist if you don't follow my advice in this matter." The analyst's voice had become whiny, shrill, almost hysterical. Lee wasn't listening; he felt a deep trust in the doctor. The doctor would take care of him. He turned to the doctor with a little-boy smile.

"Why don't you fix it yourself?"

"I haven't practiced since my internship, and I don't have the necessary materials in any case. This has to be sewed up right, or it could get infected right on up the arm."

Lee finally agreed to go to Bellevue, for medical treatment only.

At Bellevue, Lee sat on a bench, waiting while the doctor talked to somebody. The doctor came back and led Lee to another room, where an intern sewed up the finger and put on a dressing. The doctor kept urging him to allow himself to be committed; Lee was overcome by a sudden faintness. A nurse told him to put his head back. Lee felt that he must put himself entirely in the care of the doctor.

"All right," he said. "I'll do what you say."

The doctor patted his arm. "Ah, you're doing the right thing, Bill." The doctor led him past several desks, where he signed papers.

"I'm cutting red tape by the yard," the doctor said.

Finally Lee found himself in a dressing gown in a bare ward.

"Where is my room?" he asked a nurse.

"Your room! I don't know what bed you've been assigned to. Anyway you can't go there before eight unless you have a special order from the doctor."

"Where is my doctor?"

"Doctor Bromfield? He isn't here now. He'll be in tomorrow morning around ten."

"I mean Doctor Horowitz."

"Doctor Horowitz? I don't think he's on the staff here."

He looked around him at the bare corridors, the men walking around in bathrobes, muttering under the cold, indifferent eyes of an attendant.

Why, this is the psychopathic ward, he thought. *He put me in here and went away!*

———

Years later, Lee would tell the story: "Did I ever tell you about the time I got on a Van Gogh kick and cut off the end joint of my little finger?" At this point he would hold up his left hand. "This girl, see? She lives in the next room to me in a rooming house on Jane Street. That's in the Village. I love her and she's so stupid I can't make any impression. Night after night I lay there hearing her carry on with some man in the next room. It's tearing me all apart. . . . So I hit on this finger joint gimmick. I'll present it to her: 'A trifling memento of my undying affection. I suggest you wear it around your neck in a pendant filled with formaldehyde.'

"But my analyst, the lousy bastard, shanghaied me into the nuthouse, and the finger joint was sent to Potter's Field with a death certificate, because someone might find the finger joint and the police go around looking for the rest of the body.

"If you ever have occasion to cut off a finger joint, my dear, don't consider any instrument but poultry shears. That way you're sure of cutting *through* at the joint."

"And what about the girl?"

"Oh, by the time I got out of the nuthouse she'd gone to Chicago. I never saw her again."

DRIVING LESSON

The red-light district of East St. Louis is a string of wood houses along the railroad tracks: a marginal district of vacant lots, decaying billboards and cracked sidewalks where weeds grow through the cracks. Here and there you see rows of corn.

Bill and Jack were drinking in a bar on one corner of the district. They had been drinking since early afternoon, and were past the point of showing signs of drunkenness. Through the door, Bill could hear frogs croaking from pools of stagnant water in the vacant lots. Above the bar was a picture of Custer's Last Stand, distributed by courtesy of Anheuser-Busch. Bill knew the picture was valuable, like a wooden Indian. He was trying to explain this to the bartender, how an object gets rare and then valuable, the value increasing geometrically as collectors buy it up.

"Yeah," the bartender said, "you already told me that ten times. Anything else?" He walked to the other end of the bar and studied a *Racing Form*, writing on a slip of paper with a short indelible pencil.

Jack picked up a dollar of Bill's money off the bar. "I want to go in one of these houses," he said.

"All right . . . enjoy yourself." Bill watched Jack as he walked through the swinging door.

On the way back to St. Louis, Bill stopped the car.

"Want to try driving a bit?" he asked. "After all, you'll never get anywhere sitting on your ass. I remember when I was a reporter on the *St. Louis News,* my city editor sent me out to get a picture of some character committed suicide or something. . . . I forget. . . . Anyway, I couldn't get the picture. Some female relative came to the door and said, 'It would be a mockery,' and they wouldn't give me the picture.

"And next morning I went in the john and there is the city editor taking his morning crap. So he asks me: 'You got that picture, Morton?' And I said, 'No, I couldn't get it—at least not yet.'

" 'Well,' he says, 'you'll never get anywhere sitting on your ass.'

"So I start laughing, because that's exactly what he is doing, sitting on his ass, shitting. And I'll stack that up against any biographical anecdote for tasteless stupidity."

Jack looked at Bill blankly, and then laughed. *The plain truth is, he's bone stupid,* Bill thought. He opened the door and got out and walked around the car, through the headlights, and got in the other side. Jack slid in under the wheel, looking dubiously at the gadgets in front of him. He had only driven twice before in his life, both times in Bill's car.

"Oh, it's quite simple," Bill said. "You learn by doing. Could you learn to play piano by reading a book about it? Certainly not." He suddenly took Jack's chin in his hand and, turning Jack's face, kissed him lightly on the mouth. Jack laughed, showing sharp little eyeteeth.

"I always say people have more fun than anybody," Jack said.

Bill shuddered in the summer night. "I suppose they do," he said. "Well, let's get this show on the road."

Jack started the car with a grinding of gears. The car bucked, almost stopped, shot forward. Finally he got it in high and moving at an even speed.

"You'll never learn this way," Bill said. "Let's see a little speed."

It was three o'clock in the morning. Not a car on the street, not a sound. A pocket of immobile silence.

"A little speed, Jackie." Bill's voice was the eerie, disembodied voice of a young child. "That thing under your foot—push it on into the floor, Jackie."

The car gathered speed, tires humming on asphalt. There was no other sound from outside.

"We have the city all to ourselves, Jackie . . . not a car on the street. Push it all the way down . . . all the way in . . . all the way, Jackie."

Jack's face was blank, oblivious, the beautiful mouth a little open. Bill lit a cigarette from the dashboard lighter, muttering a denunciation of car lighters and car clocks. A piece of burning tobacco fell on his thigh, and he brushed it away petulantly. He looked at Jack's face and put the cigarettes away.

The car had moved into a dream beyond contact with the lives, forces and objects of the city. They were alone, safe, floating in the summer night, a moon spinning around the world. The dashboard shone like a fireplace, lighting the two young faces: one weak and beautiful, with a beauty that would show every day that much older; the other thin, intense, reflecting unmistakably the qualities loosely covered by the word "intellectual," at the same time with the look of a tormented, trapped animal. The speedometer crept up . . . 50 . . . 60 . . .

"You're learning fast, Jackie. Just keep your right foot on the floor. It's quite simple, really."

Jack swerved to avoid the metal mounds of a safety zone. The car hit a wet spot where the street had been watered and went into a long skid. There was a squealing crash of metal. Bill flew out of the car door and slid across the asphalt. He got up and ran his hands over his thin body—nothing broken. Somebody was holding his arm.

"Are you hurt, kid?"

"I don't think so."

He remembered seeing his car hauled away by a wrecker, the front wheels off the ground. He kept asking, "Where is Jack?" Finally he saw Jack with two cops. Jack looked dazed. There was a bruise on his forehead, standing out sharply on the white skin.

They rode in a police car to the hospital, where the doctor put a patch on Jack's forehead. He found a cut on Bill's leg, and swabbed it with Mercurochrome.

At the police station, Bill asked to call his father. It seemed to Bill literally no time before his father appeared, conjured by an alcoholic time trick. Suddenly there he was, cool and distant as always, talking to the cops. They had hit a parked car. The owner of the other car was there.

"So I met my wife at the train and took her to see the new car, and there wasn't any car. All four wheels knocked off."

"That will all be taken care of," Mr. Morton told him.

"Well, I should think so. That car can't be fixed. There's nothing left of it."

"In that case you will get a new car."

"Well, I should think so! People driving like that should be in jail. Endangering people's lives!" He glared at Bill and Jack.

One of the cops looked at him coldly. "We'll decide who to put in jail, mister. The gentleman is getting you a new car. What are you kicking about?"

"Well, so long as I get a new car."

There was an exchange of cards and arrangements. The desk sergeant accepted one of Mr. Morton's cigars and shook hands with him. No one paid any attention to the owner of the other car.

Bill and Jack walked out of the station with Mr. Morton.

"Where do you want to be dropped off?" Mr. Morton asked Jack. Jack told him. He got out at his street, and Bill said, "Good night, Jack. I'll give you a ring."

Jack said, "Thank you, Mr. Morton." Mr. Morton shifted his cigar without answering. He put the car in gear and drove away.

It was a long ride to the Mortons' house in the suburbs. Father and son rode in silence. Finally Bill said, "I'm sorry, Dad . . . I—"

"So am I," his father cut in.

When they reached the garage door, Bill got out and opened it, closing it again behind the car after Mr. Morton got out. Mr. Morton opened the door with a key in a leather folder. They entered the house in silence.

"It's all right, Mother," Mr. Morton called upstairs. "Nobody hurt." He started toward the pantry. "Want some milk, Bill?"

"No, thanks, Dad."

Bill went upstairs to bed.

THE JUNKY'S CHRISTMAS

It was Christmas Day and Danny the Car Wiper hit the street junk-sick and broke after seventy-two hours in the precinct jail. It was a clear bright day, but there was no warmth in the sun. Danny shivered with an inner cold. He turned up the collar of his worn, greasy black overcoat.

This beat benny wouldn't pawn for a deuce, he thought.

He was in the West Nineties. A long block of brownstone rooming houses. Here and there a holy wreath in a clean black window. Danny's senses registered everything sharp and clear, with the painful intensity of junk sickness. The light hurt his dilated eyes.

He walked past a car, darting his pale blue eyes sideways in quick appraisal. There was a package on the seat and one of the ventilator windows was unlocked. Danny walked on ten feet. No one in sight. He snapped his fingers and went through a pantomime of remembering something, and wheeled around. No one.

A bad setup, he decided. *The street being empty like this, I stand out conspicuous. Gotta make it fast.*

He reached for the ventilator window. A door opened behind him. Danny whipped out a rag and began polishing the car windows. He could feel the man standing behind him.

"What're yuh doin'?"

Danny turned as if surprised. "Just thought your car windows needed polishing, mister."

The man had a frog face and a Deep South accent. He was wearing a camel's-hair overcoat.

"My caah don't need polishin' or nothing stole out of it neither."

Danny slid sideways as the man grabbed for him. "I wasn't lookin' to steal nothing, mister. I'm from the South too. Florida—"

"Goddamned sneakin' thief!"

Danny walked away fast and turned a corner.

Better get out of the neighborhood. That hick is likely to call the law.

He walked fifteen blocks. Sweat ran down his body. There was a raw ache in his lungs. His lips drew back off his yellow teeth in a snarl of desperation.

I gotta score somehow. If I had some decent clothes . . .

Danny saw a suitcase standing in a doorway. Good leather. He stopped and pretended to look for a cigarette.

Funny, he thought. *No one around. Inside maybe, phoning for a cab.*

The corner was only a few houses away. Danny took a deep

breath and picked up the suitcase. He made the corner. Another block, another corner. The case was heavy.

I got a score here all right, he thought. *Maybe enough for a sixteenth and a room.* Danny shivered and twitched, feeling a warm room and heroin emptying into his vein. *Let's have a quick look.*

He stepped into Morningside Park. No one around.

Jesus, I never see the town this empty.

He opened the suitcase. Two long packages in brown wrapping paper. He took one out. It felt like meat. He tore the package open at one end, revealing a woman's naked foot. The toenails were painted with purple-red polish. He dropped the leg with a sneer of disgust.

"Holy Jesus!" he exclaimed. "The routines people put down these days. Legs! Well, I got a case anyway." He dumped the other leg out. No bloodstains. He snapped the case shut and walked away.

"Legs!" he muttered.

He found the Buyer sitting at a table in Jarrow's Cafeteria.

"Thought you might be taking the day off," Danny said, putting the case down.

The Buyer shook his head sadly. "I got nobody. So what's Christmas to me?" His eyes traveled over the case, poking, testing, looking for flaws. "What was in it?"

"Nothing."

"What's the matter? I don't pay enough?"

"I tell you there wasn't nothing in it."

"Okay. So somebody travels with an empty suitcase. Okay." He held up three fingers.

"For Christ's sake, Gimpy, give me a nickel."

"You got somebody else. Why don't he give you a nickel?"

"It's like I say, the case was empty."

Gimpy kicked at the case disparagingly. "It's all nicked up and kinda dirty-looking." He sniffed suspiciously. "How come it stink like that? Mexican leather?"

"So am I in the leather business?"

Gimpy shrugged. "Could be." He pulled out a roll of bills and peeled off three ones, dropping them on the table behind the napkin dispenser. "You want?"

"Okay." Danny picked up the money. "You see George the Greek?" he asked.

"Where you been? He got busted two days ago."

"Oh . . . That's bad."

Danny walked out. *Now where can I score?* he thought. George the Greek had lasted so long, Danny thought of him as permanent. *It was good H too, and no short counts.*

Danny went up to 103rd and Broadway. Nobody in Jarrow's. Nobody in the Automat.

"Yeah," he snarled. "All the pushers off on the nod someplace. What they care about anybody else? So long as they get it in the vein. What they care about a sick junky?"

He wiped his nose with one finger, looking around furtively.

No use hitting those jigs in Harlem. Like as not get beat for my money or they slip me rat poison. Might find Pantopon Rose at Eighth and 23rd.

There was no one he knew in the 23rd Street Thompson's.

Jesus, he thought. *Where is everybody?*

He clutched his coat collar together with one hand, looking up and down the street. *There's Joey from Brooklyn. I'd know that hat anywhere.*

"Joey. Hey, Joey!"

Joey was walking away, with his back to Danny. He turned around. His face was sunken, skull-like. The gray eyes glittered under a greasy gray felt hat. Joey was sniffing at regular intervals and his eyes were watering.

No use asking him, Danny thought. They looked at each other with the hatred of disappointment.

"Guess you heard about George the Greek," Danny said.

"Yeah. I heard. You been up to 103rd?"

"Yeah. Just came from there. Nobody around."

"Nobody around anyplace," Joey said. "I can't even score for goofballs."

"Well, Merry Christmas, Joey. See you."

"Yeah. See you."

Danny was walking fast. He had remembered a croaker on 18th Street. Of course the croaker had told him not to come back. Still, it was worth trying.

A brownstone house with a card in the window: *P.H. Zunniga, M.D.* Danny rang the bell. He heard slow steps. The door opened, and the doctor looked at Danny with bloodshot brown eyes. He was weaving slightly and supported his plump body against the doorjamb. His face was smooth, Latin, the little red mouth slack. He said nothing. He just leaned there, looking at Danny.

Goddamned alcoholic, Danny thought. He smiled.

"Merry Christmas, Doctor."

The doctor did not reply.

"You remember me, Doctor." Danny tried to edge past the doctor, into the house. "I'm sorry to trouble you on Christmas Day, but I've suffered another attack."

"Attack?"

"Yes. Facial neuralgia." Danny twisted one side of his face into a horrible grimace. The doctor recoiled slightly, and Danny pushed into the dark hallway.

"Better shut the door or you'll be catching cold," he said jovially, shoving the door shut.

The doctor looked at him, his eyes focusing visibly. "I can't give you a prescription," he said.

"But Doctor, this is a legitimate condition. An emergency, you understand."

"No prescription. Impossible. It's against the law."

"You took an oath, Doctor. I'm in agony." Danny's voice shot up to a hysterical grating whine.

The doctor winced and passed a hand over his forehead.

"Let me think. I can give you one quarter-grain tablet. That's all I have in the house."

"But, Doctor—a quarter G . . ."

The doctor stopped him. "If your condition is legitimate, you will not need more. If it isn't, I don't want anything to do with you. Wait right here."

The doctor weaved down the hall, leaving a wake of alcoholic breath. He came back and dropped a tablet into Danny's hand. Danny wrapped the tablet in a piece of paper and tucked it away.

"There is no charge." The doctor put his hand on the doorknob. "And now, my dear . . ."

"But, Doctor—can't you inject the medication?"

"No. You will obtain longer relief in using orally. Please not to return." The doctor opened the door.

Well, this will take the edge off, and I still have money to put down on a room, Danny thought.

He knew a drugstore that sold needles without question. He bought a 26-gauge insulin needle and an eyedropper, which he selected carefully, rejecting models with a curved dropper or a thick end. Finally he bought a baby pacifier, to use instead of the bulb. He stopped in the Automat and stole a teaspoon.

Danny put down two dollars on a six-dollar-a-week room in the West Forties, where he knew the landlord. He bolted the door and put his spoon, needle and dropper on a table by the bed. He dropped the tablet in the spoon and covered it with a dropperful of water. He held a match under the spoon until the tablet dissolved. He tore a strip of paper, wet it and wrapped it around the end of the dropper, fitting the needle over the wet paper to make an airtight connection. He dropped a piece of lint from his pocket into the spoon and sucked the liquid into the dropper through the needle, holding the needle in the lint to take up the last drop.

Danny's hands trembled with excitement and his breath was quick. With a shot in front of him, his defenses gave way, and junk sickness flooded his body. His legs began to twitch and ache. A cramp stirred in his stomach. Tears ran down his face from his smarting, burning eyes. He wrapped a handkerchief around his right arm, holding the end in his teeth. He tucked the handkerchief in, and began rubbing his arm to bring out a vein.

Guess I can hit that one, he thought, running one finger along a vein. He picked up the dropper in his left hand.

Danny heard a groan from the next room. He frowned with annoyance. Another groan. He could not help listening. He walked across the room, the dropper in his hand, and inclined his ear to the wall. The groans were coming at regular intervals, a horrible inhuman sound pushed out from the stomach.

Danny listened for a full minute. He returned to the bed and sat down. *Why don't someone call a doctor?* he thought indignantly. *It's a bringdown.* He straightened his arm and poised the needle. He tilted his head, listening again.

Oh, for Christ's sake! He tore off the handkerchief and placed the dropper in a water glass, which he hid behind the wastebasket. He stepped into the hall and knocked on the door of the next room. There was no answer. The groans continued. Danny tried the door. It was open.

The shade was up and the room was full of light. He had expected an old person somehow, but the man on the bed was very young, eighteen or twenty, fully clothed and doubled up, with his hands clasped across his stomach.

"What's wrong, kid?" Danny asked.

The boy looked at him, his eyes blank with pain. Finally he got out one word: "Kidneys."

"Kidney stones?" Danny smiled. "I don't mean it's funny, kid. It's just . . . I've faked it so many times. Never saw the real thing before. I'll call an ambulance."

The boy bit his lip. "Won't come. Doctors won't come." The boy hid his face in the pillow.

Danny nodded. "They figure it's just another junky throwing a wingding for a shot. But your case is legit. Maybe if I went to the hospital and explained things . . . No, I guess that wouldn't be so good."

"Don't live here," the boy said, his voice muffled. "They say I'm not entitled."

"Yeah, I know how they are, the bureaucrat bastards. I had a friend once, died of snakebite right in the waiting room. They wouldn't even listen when he tried to explain a snake bit him. He never had enough moxie. That was fifteen years ago, down in Jacksonville. . . ."

Danny trailed off. Suddenly he put out his thin, dirty hand and touched the boy's shoulder.

"I—I'm sorry, kid. You wait. I'll fix you up."

He went back to his room and got the dropper, and returned to the boy's room.

"Roll up your sleeve, kid." The boy fumbled his coat sleeve with a weak hand.

"That's okay. I'll get it." Danny undid the shirt button at the wrist and pushed the shirt and coat up, baring a thin brown forearm. Danny hesitated, looking at the dropper. Sweat ran down his nose. The boy was looking up at him. Danny shoved the needle in the boy's forearm and watched the liquid drain into the flesh. He straightened up.

The boy's face began to relax. He sat up and smiled.

"Say, that stuff really works," he said. "You a doctor, mister?"

"No, kid."

The boy lay down, stretching. "I feel real sleepy. Didn't sleep all last night." His eyes were closing.

Danny walked across the room and pulled the shade down. He went back to his room and closed the door without locking it. He sat on the bed, looking at the empty dropper. It was getting dark outside. Danny's body ached for junk, but it was a dull ache now, dull and hopeless. Numbly, he took the needle off the dropper and wrapped it in a piece of paper. Then he wrapped the needle and dropper together. He sat there with the package in his hand. *Gotta stash this someplace*, he thought.

Suddenly a warm flood pulsed through his veins and broke in his head like a thousand golden speedballs.

For Christ's sake, Danny thought. *I must have scored for the immaculate fix!*

The vegetable serenity of junk settled in his tissues. His face went slack and peaceful, and his head fell forward.

Danny the Car Wiper was on the nod.

LEE AND THE BOYS

The sun spotlights the inner thigh of a boy sitting in shorts on a doorstep, his legs swinging open, and you fall in spasms—sperm spurting in orgasm after orgasm, grinding against the stone street, neck and back break . . . now lying dead, eyes rolled back, showing slits of white that redden slowly, as blood tears form and run down the face—

Or the sudden clean smell of salt air, piano down a city street, a dusty poplar tree shaking in the hot afternoon wind, pictures explode in the brain like skyrockets, smells, tastes, sounds shake the body, nostalgia becomes unendurable, aching pain, the brain is an overloaded switchboard sending insane messages and countermessages to the viscera. Finally the body gives up, cowering like a neurotic cat, blood pressure drops, body fluids leak through stretched, flaccid veins, shock passes to coma and death.

Somebody rapped on the outside shutter. Lee opened the shutter and looked out. An Arab boy of fourteen or so—they always look younger than they are—was standing there, smiling in a way that could only mean one thing. He said something in Spanish that Lee did not catch. Lee shook his head and started to close the shutter. The boy, still smiling, held the shutter open. Lee gave a jerk and slammed the shutter closed. He could feel the rough wood catch and tear the boy's hand. The boy turned without a word and walked away, his shoulders drooping, holding his hand. At the corner the small figure caught a patch of light.

I didn't mean to hurt him, Lee thought. He wished he had given the boy some money, a smile at least. He felt crude and detestable.

Years ago he had been riding in a hotel station wagon in the West Indies. The station wagon slowed down for a series of bumps, and a little black girl ran up smiling and threw a bouquet of flowers into the car through the rear window. A round-faced, heavyset American in a brown gabardine suit gathered up the flowers and said, "No want," and tossed them at the little girl. The flowers fell in the dusty road, and the little girl turned around crying and ran away.

Lee closed the shutter slowly.

In the Rio Grande valley of South Texas, he had killed a rattlesnake with a golf club. The impact of metal on the live flesh of the snake sent an electric shiver through him.

In New York, when he was rolling lushes on the subway with Roy, at the end of the line in Brooklyn a drunk grabbed Roy and started yelling for the law. Lee hit the drunk in the face and knocked him to his knees, then kicked him in the side. A rib snapped. Lee felt a shudder of nausea.

Next day he told Roy he was through as a lush worker. Roy looked at him with his impersonal brown eyes that caught points of light, like an opal. There was a masculine gentleness in Roy's voice, a gentleness that only the strong have: "You feel bad about kicking that mooch, don't you? You're not cut out for this sort of thing, Bill. I'll find someone else to work with." Roy put on his hat and started to leave. He stopped with the doorknob in his hand and turned around.

"It's none of my business, Bill. But you have enough money to get by. Why don't you just quit?" He walked out without waiting for Lee to answer.

Lee did not feel like finishing the letter. He put on his coat and stepped out into the narrow, sunless street.

The druggist saw Lee standing in the doorway of the store. The store was about eight feet wide, with bottles and packages packed around three walls. The druggist smiled and held up a finger.

"One?" he said in English.

Lee nodded, looking around at the bottles and packages. The clerk handed the box of ampules to Lee without wrapping it. Lee said, "Thank you."

He walked away through a street lined on both sides with bazaars. Merchandise overflowed into the street, and he dodged crockery and washtubs and trays of combs and pencils and soap dishes. A train of burros loaded with charcoal blocked his way. He passed a woman with no nose, a black slit in her face, her body wrapped in grimy, padded pink cotton. Lee walked fast, twisting his body sideways, squeezing past people. He reached the sunny alleys of the outer Medina.

Walking in Tangier was like falling, plunging down dark shafts of streets, catching at corners, doorways. He passed a blind man sitting in the sun in a doorway. The man was young, with a fringe of blond beard. He sat there with one hand out, his shirt open, showing the smooth, patient flesh, the slight, immobile folds in the stomach. He sat there all day, every day.

Lee turned into his street, and a cool wind from the sea chilled the sweat on his thin body. He hooked the key into the lock and pushed the door open with his shoulder.

He tied up for the shot, and slid the needle in through a festered scab. Blood swirled up into the hypo—he was using a regular hypo these days. He pressed the plunger down with his forefinger. A passing caress of pleasure flushed through his veins. He glanced at the cheap alarm clock on the table by the bed: four o'clock. He was meeting his boy at eight. Time enough for the Eukodal to get out of his system.

Lee walked about the room. "I have to quit," he said over and over, feeling the gravity pull of junk in his cells. He experienced a moment of panic. A cry of despair wrenched his body: "I have to get *out* of here. I have to make a break."

As he said the words, he remembered whose words they were: the Mad Dog Esposito Brothers, arrested at the scene of a multiple-slaying holdup, separated from the electric chair by a little time and a few formalities, whispered these words into a police microphone planted by their beds in the detention ward.

He sat down at the typewriter, yawned, and made some notes on a separate piece of paper. Lee often spent hours on a letter. He dropped the pencil and stared at the wall, his face blank and dreamy, reflecting on the heartwarming picture of William Lee—

He was sure the reviewers in those queer magazines like *One* would greet Willy Lee as heartwarming, except when he gets— squirming uneasily—well, you know, a bit out of line, somehow.

"Oh, that's just boyishness—after all, you know a boy's will is the wind's will, and the thoughts of youth are long, long thoughts."

"Yes I know, but . . . the purple-assed baboons . . ."

"That's gangrened innocence."

"Why didn't I think of *that* myself. And the piles?"

"All kids are like hung up on something."

"So they are . . . and the prolapsed assholes feeling around, looking for a peter, like blind worms?"

"Schoolboy smut."

"Understand, I'm not trying to *belittle* Lee—"

"You'd better not. He's a one-hundred-percent wistful boy, listening to train whistles across the winter stubble and frozen red clay of Georgia."

—yes, there was something a trifle disquieting in the fact that the heartwarming picture of William Lee should be drawn by William Lee himself. He thought of the ultimate development in stooges, a telepathic stooge who tunes in on your psyche and says just what you want to hear: "Boss, you is heartwarming. You is a latter-assed purple-day saint."

Lee put down the pencil and yawned. He looked at the bed.

I'm sleepy, he decided. He took off his pants and shoes and lay down on the bed, covering himself with a cotton blanket. *They don't scratch*. He closed his eyes. Pictures streamed by, the magic lantern of junk. There is a feeling of too much junk that corresponds to the bed spinning around when you are very drunk, a feeling of gray, dead horror. The pictures in the brain are out of control, black and white, without emotion, the deadness of junk lying in the body like a viscous, thick medium.

A child came up to Lee and held up to him a bleeding hand.

"Who did this?" Lee asked. "I'll kill him. Who did it?"

The child beckoned Lee into a dark room. He pointed at Lee with the bleeding stub of a finger. Lee woke up crying "No! No!"

Lee looked at the clock. It was almost eight. His boy was due anytime. Lee rummaged in a drawer of the bed table and found a stick of tea. He lit it and lay back to wait for KiKi. There was a bitter, green taste in his mouth from the weed. He could feel a warm tingle spread over his body. He put his hands behind his head, stretching his ribs and arching his stomach.

Lee was forty, but he had the lean body of an adolescent. He looked down at the stomach, which curved in flat from the chest. Junk had sculpted his body down to bone and muscle. He could feel the wall of his stomach right under the skin. His skin smooth and white, he looked almost transparent, like a tropical fish, with blue veins where the hipbones protruded.

KiKi stepped in. He switched on the light.

"Sleeping?" he asked.

"No, just resting." Lee got up and put his arms around KiKi, holding him in a long, tight embrace.

"What's the matter, Meester William?" KiKi said, laughing.

"Nothing."

They sat down on the edge of the bed. KiKi ran his hands absently over Lee's back. He turned and looked at Lee.

"Very thin," he said. "You should eat more."

Lee pulled in his stomach so it almost touched the backbone. KiKi laughed and ran his hands down Lee's ribs to the stomach. He put his thumbs on Lee's backbone and tried to encircle Lee's stomach with his hands. He got up and took off his clothes and sat down beside Lee, caressing him with casual affection.

Like many Spanish boys, KiKi did not feel love for women. To him a woman was only for sex. He had known Lee for some months, and felt a genuine fondness for him, in an offhand way. Lee was considerate and generous and did not ask KiKi to do things he didn't want to do, leaving the lovemaking on an adolescent basis. KiKi was well pleased with the arrangement.

And Lee was well pleased with KiKi. He did not like the process of looking for boys. He did not lose interest in a boy after a few contacts, not being subject to compulsive promiscuity. In Mexico he had slept with the same boy twice a week for over a year. The boy had looked enough like KiKi to be his brother. Both had very straight black hair, an Oriental look, and lean, slight bodies. Both exuded the same quality of sweet masculine innocence. Lee met the same people wherever he went.

IN THE CAFÉ CENTRAL

Johnny the Guide was sitting in front of the Café Central with Mrs. Merrims and her sixteen-year-old son. Mrs. Merrims was traveling on her husband's insurance. She was well-groomed and competent. She was making out a list of purchases and places to go. Johnny leaned forward, solicitous and deferential.

The other guides cruised by like frustrated sharks. Johnny savored their envy. His eyes slid sideways over the lean adolescent body of the boy, poised in gray flannels and a sport shirt open at the neck. Johnny licked his lips.

Hans sat several tables away. He was a German who procured

boys for English and American visitors. He had a house in the native quarter—bed and boy, two dollars per night. But most of his clients went in for "quickies." Hans had typical Nordic features, with heavy bone structure. There was something skull-like in his face.

Morton Christie was sitting with Hans. Morton was a pathetic name-dropper and table-hopper. Hans was the only one in Tangier who could stand his silly chatter, his interminable dull lies about wealth and social prominence. One story involved two aunts, living in a house together, who hadn't spoken to each other in twenty years.

"But you see, the house is so huge that it doesn't matter, really. They each have their own set of servants and maintain completely separate households."

Hans just sat there and smiled through all of these stories. "It is a little girl," he would say in defense of Morton. "You must not be hard with him."

Actually Morton had, through years of insecurity—sitting at tables where he wasn't wanted, desperately attempting to gain a moment's reprieve from dismissal—gained an acute sense for gossip and scandal. If someone was down with the clap, Morton always found out somehow. He had a sense for anything anyone was trying to conceal. The most perfect poker face was no protection against this telepathic penetration.

Besides, without being a good listener, sympathetic, or in any way someone you would want to confide in, he had a way of surprising confidences out of you. Sometimes you forgot he was there and said something to someone else at the table. Sometimes he would slip in a question, personal, impertinent, but you answered him before you knew it. His personality was so negative there was nothing to put you on guard. Hans found Morton's talent for collecting information useful. He could find out what was happening in town by spending half an hour listening to Morton in the Café Central.

Morton had literally no self-respect, so that his self-esteem went up or down in accordance with how others felt about him. At first he often made a good impression. He appeared naïve, boyish, friendly. Imperceptibly the naïveté degenerated into silly, mechanical chatter, his friendliness into compulsive, clinging hunger, and his boyishness faded before your eyes across a café table. You looked up and saw the deep lines about the mouth, a hard, stupid mouth like an old whore's, you saw the deep creases in the back of the neck when he craned around to look at somebody—he was always looking around restlessly, as if he were waiting for someone more important than whomever he was sitting with.

There were, to be sure, people who engaged his whole attention. He twisted in hideous convulsions of ingratiation, desperate as he saw every pitiful attempt fail flatly, often shitting in his pants with fear and excitement. Lee wondered if he went home and sobbed with despair.

Morton's attempts to please socially prominent residents and visiting celebrities, ending usually in flat failure, or a snub in the Café Central, attracted a special sort of scavenger who feeds on the humiliation and disintegration of others. These decayed queens never tired of retailing the endless saga of Morton's social failures.

"So he sat *right down* with Tennessee Williams on the beach, and Tennessee said to him: 'I'm not feeling well this morning, *Michael*. I'd rather not talk to anybody.' '*Michael!*' Doesn't even know his *name!* And he says, 'Oh yes, Tennessee is a good friend of mine!' " And they would laugh, and throw themselves around and flip their wrists, their eyes glowing with loathsome lust.

I imagine that's the way people look when they watch someone burned at the stake, Lee thought.

At another table was a beautiful woman, of mixed Negro and

Malay stock. She was delicately proportioned, with a dark, copper-colored complexion and small teeth set far apart, her nipples pointed a little upward. She was dressed in a yellow silk gown and carried herself with superb grace. At the same table sat a German woman with perfect features: golden hair curled in braids forming a tiara, a magnificent bust, and heroic proportions.

She was talking to the half-caste. When she opened her mouth to speak, she revealed horrible teeth, gray, carious, repaired rather than filled with pieces of steel—some actually rusty, others of copper covered with green verdigris. The teeth were abnormally large and crowded over each other. Broken, corroded braces stuck to them, like an old barbed-wire fence.

Ordinarily she attempted to keep her teeth covered as far as possible. However, her beautiful mouth was hardly adequate to perform this function, and the teeth peeked out here and there as she talked or ate. She never laughed if she could help it, but was subject to occasional laughing jags brought on by apparently random circumstances. The laughing jags were always followed by fits of crying, during which she would repeat over and over, "Everybody saw my teeth! My horrible teeth!"

She was constantly saving up money to have the teeth out, but somehow she always spent the money on something else. Either she got drunk on it, or she gave it to someone in an irrational fit of generosity. She was a mark for every con artist in Tangier, because she was known to have the money she was always saving up to have her teeth out. But putting the touch on her was not without danger. She would suddenly turn vicious and maul some mooch with all the strength of her Junoesque limbs, shouting, "You lousy bastard! Trying to con me out of my teeth money!"

Both the half-caste and the Nordic, who had taken on herself the name of Helga, were free-lance whores.

DREAM OF THE
PENAL COLONY

That night Lee dreamed he was in a penal colony. All around were high, bare mountains. He lived in a boardinghouse that was never warm. He went out for a walk. As he stepped off the street corner onto a dirty cobblestone street, the cold mountain wind hit him. He tightened the belt of a leather jacket and felt the chill of final despair.

Nobody talks much after the first few years in the colony, because they know the others are in identical conditions of misery. They sit at table, eating the cold, greasy food, separate and silent as

43

stones. Only the whiny, penetrating voice of the landlady goes on and on.

The colonists mix with the townspeople, and it is difficult to pick them out. But sooner or later they betray themselves by a misplaced intensity, which derives from the exclusive preoccupation with escape. There is also the penal-colony look: control, without inner calm or balance; bitter knowledge, without maturity; intensity, without warmth or love.

The colonists know that any spontaneous expression of feeling brings the harshest punishment. Provocative agents continually mix with the prisoners, saying, "Relax. Be yourself. Express your real feelings." Lee was convinced that the means to escape lay through a relationship with one of the townspeople, and to that end he frequented the cafés.

One day he was sitting in the Metropole opposite a young man. The young man was talking about his childhood in a coastal town. Lee sat staring through the boy's head, seeing the salt marshes, the red-brick houses, the old rusty barge by the inlet where the boys took off their clothes to swim.

This may be it, Lee thought. *Easy now. Cool, cool. Don't scare him off.* Lee's stomach knotted with excitement.

During the following week, Lee tried every approach he knew, shamelessly throwing aside unsuccessful routines with a shrug: "I was only kidding," or, "*Son cosas de la vida.*" He descended to the most abject emotional blackmail and panhandling. When this failed, he scaled a dangerous cliff (not quite so dangerous either, since he knew every inch of the ascent) to capture a species of beautiful green lizard found only on these ledges. He gave the boy the lizard, attached to a chain of jade.

"It took me seven years to carve that chain," Lee said. Actually he had won the chain from a traveling salesman in a game of Latah. The boy was touched, and consented to go to bed with Lee, but soon afterward broke off intimate relationships. Lee was in despair.

I love him and besides, I haven't discovered the Secret. Perhaps he is an Agent. Lee looked at the boy with hatred. His face was breaking up, as if melted from inside by a blowtorch.

"Why won't you help me?" he demanded. "Do you want another lizard? I will get you a black lizard with beautiful violet eyes, that lives on the west slope where the winds pick climbers from the cliff and suck them out of crevices. There is only one other purple-eyed lizard in town and that one—well, never mind. The purple-eyed lizard is more venomous than a cobra, but he never bites his master. He is the sweetest and gentlest animal on earth. Just let me show you how sweet and gentle a purple-eyed lizard can be."

"Never mind," said the boy, laughing. "Anyhoo, one lizard is enough."

"Don't say anyhoo. Well, I will cut off my foot and shrink it down by a process I learned from the Auca, and make you a watch fob."

"What I want with your ugly old foot?"

"I will get you money for a guide and a pack train. You can return to the coast."

"I'll go back there anytime I feel like it. My brother-in-law knows the route."

The thought of someone being able to leave at will so enraged Lee that he was in danger of losing control. His sweaty hand gripped the snap-knife in his pocket.

The boy looked at him with distaste. "You look very nasty. Your face has turned all sorta black, greenish-black. Are you deliberately trying to make me sick?"

Lee turned on all the control that years of confinement had taught him. His face faded from greenish-black to mahogany, and back to its normal suntanned brown color. The control was spreading through his body like a shot of M. Lee smiled smoothly, but a muscle in his cheek twitched.

"Just an old Shipibo trick. They turn themselves black for night hunting, you understand. . . . Did I ever tell you about the time I ran out of K-Y in the headwaters of the Effendi? That was the year of the rindpest, when everything died, even the hyenas."

Lee went into one of his routines. The boy was laughing now. Lee made a dinner appointment.

"All right," said the boy. "But no more of your Shipibo tricks."

Lee laughed with easy joviality. "Gave you a turn, eh, young man? Did me too, the first time I saw it. Puked up a tapeworm. Well, good night."

INTERNATIONAL ZONE

A miasma of suspicion and snobbery hangs over the European Quarter of Tangier. Everyone looks you over for the price tag, appraising you like merchandise in terms of immediate practical or prestige advantage. The Boulevard Pasteur is the Fifth Avenue of Tangier. The store clerks tend to be discourteous unless you buy something immediately. Inquiries without purchase are coldly and grudgingly answered.

My first night in town I went to a fashionable bar, one of the few places that continues prosperous in the present slump: dim light, well-dressed androgynous clientele, reminiscent of many bars on New York's Upper East Side.

I started conversation with a man on my right. He was wearing one of those brown sackcloth jackets, the inexpensive creation of an ultra-chic Worth Avenue shop. Evidently it is the final touch of smartness to appear in a twelve-dollar jacket, the costume jewelry pattern—I happened to know just where the jacket came from and how much it cost because I had one like it in my suitcase. (A few days later I gave it to a shoeshine boy.)

The man's face was gray, puffy, set in a mold of sour discontent, *rich* discontent. It's an expression you see more often on women, and if a woman sits there long enough with that expression of rich discontent and sourness, a Cadillac simply builds itself around her. A man would probably accrete a Jaguar. Come to think, I had seen a Jaguar parked outside the bar.

The man answered my questions in cautious, short sentences, carefully deleting any tinge of warmth or friendliness.

"Did you come here direct from the States?" I persisted.

"No. From Brazil."

He's warming up, I thought. I expected it would take two sentences to elicit that much information.

"So? And how did you come?"

"By yacht, *of course.*"

I felt that anything would be an anticlimax after that, and allowed my shaky option on his notice to lapse.

The European Quarter of Tangier contains a surprising number of first-class French and international restaurants, where excellent food is served at very reasonable prices. Sample menu at The Alhambra, one of the best French restaurants: Snails *à la bourgogne*, one half partridge with peas and potatoes, a frozen chocolate mousse, a selection of French cheeses, and fruit. Price: one dollar. This price and menu can be duplicated in ten or twelve other restaurants.

Walking downhill from the European Quarter, we come, by inexorable process of suction, to the Socco Chico—Little Market—which is no longer a market at all but simply a paved rectangle about a block long, lined on both sides with shops and cafés. The Café Central, by reason of a location that allows the best view of the most people passing through the Socco, is the official meeting place of the Socco Chico set. Cars are barred from the Socco between 8 A.M. and 12 midnight. Often groups without money to order coffee will stand for hours in the Socco, talking. During the day they can sit in front of the cafés without ordering, but from 5 to 8 P.M. they must relinquish their seats to paying clients, unless they can strike up a conversation with a group of payers.

The Socco Chico is the meeting place, the nerve center, the switchboard of Tangier. Practically everyone in town shows there once a day at least. Many residents of Tangier spend most of their waking hours in the Socco. On all sides you see men washed up here in hopeless, dead-end situations, waiting for job offers, acceptance checks, visas, permits that will never come. All their lives they have drifted with an unlucky current, always taking the wrong turn. Here they are. This is it. Last stop: the Socco Chico of Tangier.

The market of psychic exchange is as glutted as the shops. A nightmare feeling of stasis permeates the Socco, like nothing can happen, nothing can change. Conversations disintegrate in cosmic inanity. People sit at café tables, silent and separate as stones. No other relation than physical closeness is possible. Economic laws, untouched by any human factor, evolve equations of ultimate stasis. Someday the young Spaniards in gabardine trench coats talking about soccer, the Arab guides and hustlers pitching pennies and smoking their *keif* pipes, the perverts sitting in front of the cafés looking over the boys, the boys parading past, the mooches and pimps and smugglers and money changers, will be frozen forever in a final, meaningless posture.

Futility seems to have gained a new dimension in the Socco. Sitting at a café table, listening to some "proposition," I would suddenly realize that the other was telling a fairy story to a child, the child inside himself: pathetic fantasies of smuggling, of trafficking in diamonds, drugs, guns, of starting nightclubs, bowling alleys, travel agencies. Or sometimes there was nothing wrong with the idea, except it would never be put into practice—the crisp, confident voice, the decisive gestures, in shocking contrast to the dead, hopeless eyes, drooping shoulders, clothes beyond mending, now allowed to disintegrate undisturbed.

Some of these men have ability and intelligence, like Brinton, who writes unpublishably obscene novels and exists on a small income. He undoubtedly has talent, but his work is hopelessly unsalable. He has intelligence, the rare ability to see relations between disparate factors, to coordinate data, but he moves through life like a phantom, never able to find the time, place and person to put anything into effect, to realize any project in terms of three-dimensional reality. He could have been a successful business executive, anthropologist, explorer, criminal, but the conjuncture of circumstances was never there. He is always too late or too early. His abilities remain larval, discarnate. He is the last of an archaic line, or the first here from another space-time way—in any case a man without context, of no place and no time.

Chris, the English Public School man, is the type who gets involved in fur farming, projects to raise ramie, frogs, cultured pearls. He had, in fact, lost all his savings in a bee-raising venture in the West Indies. He had observed that all the honey was imported and expensive. It looked like a sure thing, and he invested all he had. He did not know about a certain moth preying on the bees in that area, so that bee-raising is impossible.

"The sort of thing that could only happen to Chris," his friends say, for this is one chapter in a fantastic saga of misfortune. Who but Chris would be caught short at the beginning of the war, in a total shortage of drugs, and have a molar extracted without anesthetic? On another occasion he had collapsed with peritonitis and been shanghaied into a Syrian hospital, where they never heard of penicillin. He was rescued, on the verge of death, by the English consul. During the Spanish occupation of Tangier, he had been mistaken for a Spanish Communist and held for three weeks incommunicado in a detention camp.

Now he is broke and jobless in the Socco Chico, an intelligent man, willing to work, speaking several languages fluently, yet bearing the indelible brand of bad luck and failure. He is carefully shunned by the Jaguar-driving set, who fear contagion from the mysterious frequency that makes, of men like Chris, lifelong failures. He manages to stay alive teaching English and selling whiskey on commission.

Robbins is about fifty, with the face of a Cockney informer, the archetypal "Copper's Nark." He has a knack of pitching his whiny voice directly into your consciousness. No external noise drowns him out. Robbins looks like some unsuccessful species of *Homo non sapiens*, blackmailing the human race with his existence.

"Remember me? I'm the boy you left back there with the lemurs and the baboons. I'm not equipped for survival like *some* people." He holds out his deformed hands, hideously infantile, unfinished, his greedy blue eyes searching for a spot of guilt or uncertainty, on which he will fasten like a lamprey.

Robbins had all his money in his wife's name to evade income tax, and his wife ran away with a perfidious Australian. ("And I thought he was my friend.") This is one story. Robbins has a series, all involving his fall from wealth, betrayed and cheated by dishonest associates. He fixes his eyes on you probingly, accusingly: are you another betrayer who would refuse a man a few pesetas when he is down?

Robbins also comes on with the "I can't go home" routine, hinting at dark crimes committed in his native land. Many of the

Socco Chico regulars say they can't go home, trying to mitigate the dead gray of prosaic failure with a touch of borrowed color.

As a matter of fact, if anyone was wanted for a serious crime, the authorities could get him out of Tangier in ten minutes. As for these stories of disappearing into the Native Quarter, living there only makes a foreigner that much more conspicuous. Any guide or shoeshine boy would lead the cops to your door for five pesetas or a few cigarettes. So when someone gets confidential over the third drink you have bought him and tells you he can't go home, you are hearing the classic prelude to a touch.

A Danish boy is stranded here waiting for a friend to come with money and "the rest of his luggage." Every day he meets the ferry from Gibraltar and the ferry from Algeciras. A Spanish boy is waiting for a permit to enter the French Zone (for some reason persistently denied), where his uncle will give him a job. An English boy was robbed of all his money and valuables by a girlfriend.

I have never seen so many people in one place without money, or any prospects of money. This is partly due to the fact that anyone can enter Tangier. You don't have to prove solvency. So people come here hoping to get a job, or become smugglers. But there are no jobs in Tangier, and smuggling is as overcrowded as any other line. So they end up on the bum in the Socco Chico.

All of them curse Tangier, and hope for some miracle that will deliver them from the Socco Chico. They will get a job on a yacht, they will write a best-seller, they will smuggle a thousand cases of Scotch into Spain, they will find someone to finance their roulette system. It is typical of these people that they all believe in some gambling system, usually a variation on the old routine of doubling up when you lose, which is the pattern of their lives. They always back up their mistakes with more of themselves.

Some of the Socco Chico regulars, like Chris, make a real effort to support themselves. Others are full-time professional spongers.

Antonio the Portuguese is mooch to the bone. He won't work. In a sense, he can't work. He is a mutilated fragment of the human potential, specialized to the point where he cannot exist without a host. His mere presence is an irritation. Phantom tendrils reach out from him, feeling for a point of weakness on which to fasten.

Jimmy the Dane is another full-time mooch. He has a gift for showing precisely when you don't want to see him, and saying exactly what you don't want to hear. His technique is to make you dislike him more than his actual behavior, a bit obnoxious to be sure, warrants. This makes you feel guilty toward him, so you buy him off with a drink or a few pesetas.

Some mooches specialize in tourists and transients, making no attempt to establish themselves on terms of social equality with the long-term residents. They use some variation of the short con, strictly one-time touches.

There is a Jewish mooch who looks vaguely like a detective or some form of authority. He approaches a tourist in a somewhat peremptory manner. The tourist anticipates an inspection of his passport or some other annoyance. When he finds out it is merely a question of a small "loan," he often gives the money in relief.

A young Norwegian has a routine of approaching visitors without his glass eye, a really unnerving sight. He needs money to buy a glass eye, or he will lose a job he is going to apply for in the morning. "How can I work as a waiter looking so as this?" he says, turning his empty socket on the victim. "I would frighten the customers, is it not?"

Many of the Socco Chico regulars are left over from the Boom. A few years ago the town was full of operators and spenders. There was a boom of money changing and transfer, smuggling and borderline enterprise. Restaurants and hotels turned customers away. Bars served a full house around the clock.

What happened? What gave out? What corresponds to the gold, the oil, the construction projects? Largely, inequalities in prices and exchange rates. Tangier is a clearinghouse, from which currency and merchandise move in any direction toward higher prices. Under this constant flow of goods, shortages created by the war are supplied, prices and currency approach standard rates, and Tangier is running down like the dying universe, where no movement is possible because all energy is equally distributed.

Tangier is a vast overstocked market, everything for sale and no buyers. A glut of obscure brands of Scotch, inferior German cameras and Swiss watches, second-run factory-reject nylons, typewriters unknown anywhere else, is displayed in shop after shop. There is quite simply too much of everything, too much merchandise, housing, labor, too many guides, pimps, prostitutes and smugglers. A classic, archetypical depression.

The guides of Tangier are in a class by themselves, and I have never seen their equal for insolence, persistence and all-around obnoxiousness. It is not surprising that the very word "guide" carries, in Tangier, the strongest opprobrium.

The Navy issues a bulletin on what to do if you find yourself in shark-infested waters: "Above all, avoid making uncoordinated, flailing movements that might be interpreted by a shark as the struggles of a disabled fish." The same advice might apply to keeping off guides. They are infallibly attracted by the uncoordinated movements of the tourist in a strange medium. The least show of uncertainty, of not knowing exactly where you are going, and they rush on you from their lurking places in side streets and Arab cafés.

"Want nice girl, mister?"

"See Kasbah? Sultan's Palace?"

"Want *keif*? Watch me fuck my sister?"

"Caves of Hercules? Nice boy?"

Their persistence is amazing, their impertinence unlimited. They will follow one for blocks, finally demanding a tip for the time they have wasted.

Female prostitution is largely confined to licensed houses. On the other hand, male prostitutes are everywhere. They assume that all visitors are homosexual, and solicit openly in the streets. I have been approached by boys who could not have been over twelve.

A casino would certainly bring in more tourists, and do much to alleviate the economic condition of Tangier. But despite the concerted efforts of merchants and hotel owners, all attempts to build a casino have been blocked by the Spanish on religious grounds.

Tangier has a dubious climate. The winters are cold and wet. In summer the temperature is pleasant, neither too hot nor too cool, but a constant wind creates a sandstorm on the beach, and people who sit there all day get sand in their ears and hair and eyes. Owing to a current, the water is shock-cold in mid-August, so even the hardiest swimmers can only stay in a few minutes. The beach is not much of an attraction.

All in all, Tangier does not have much to offer the visitor except low prices and a buyer's market. I have mentioned the unusually large number of good restaurants (a restaurant guide put out by the American and Foreign Bank lists eighteen first-class eating places where the price for a complete meal ranges from eighty cents to two dollars and a half). You have your choice of apartments and houses. Sample price for one large room with bath and balcony overlooking the harbor, comfortably furnished, utilities and maid service included: $25 per month. And there are comfortable rooms for $10. A tailor-made suit of imported English material that would cost $150 in the U.S. is $50 in Tangier. Name brands of Scotch run $2 to $2.50 a fifth.

Americans are exempt from the usual annoyances of registering with the police, renewing visas and so forth, that one encounters in Europe and South America. No visa is required for Tangier. You can stay as long as you want, work, if you can find a job, or go into business, without any formalities or permits. And Americans have extraterritorial rights in Tangier. Cases civil or criminal involving an American citizen are tried in consular court, under District of Columbia law.

The legal system of Tangier is rather complex. Criminal cases are tried by a mixed tribunal of three judges. Sentences are comparatively mild. Two years is usual for burglary, even if the criminal has a long record. A sentence of more than five years is extremely rare. Tangier does have capital punishment. The method is a firing squad of ten gendarmes. I know of only one case in recent years in which a death sentence was carried out.

In the Native Quarter one feels definite currents of hostility, which, however, are generally confined to muttering in Arabic as you pass. Occasionally I have been openly insulted by drunken Arabs, but this is rare. You can walk in the Native Quarter of Tangier with less danger than on Third Avenue of New York City on a Saturday night.

Violent crime is rare. I have walked the streets at all hours, and never was any attempt made to rob me. The infrequency of armed robbery is due less, I think, to the pacific nature of the Arabs than to the certainty of detection in a town where everybody knows everybody else, and where the penalties for violent crime, especially if committed by a Moslem, are relatively severe.

The Native Quarter of Tangier is all you expect it to be: a maze of narrow, sunless streets, twisting and meandering like footpaths, many of them blind alleys. After four months, I still find my way in the Medina by a system of moving from one landmark to another. The smell is almost incredible, and it is difficult to identify all the ingredients. Hashish, seared meat and sewage are well represented. You see filth, poverty, disease, all endured with a curiously apathetic indifference.

People carry huge loads of charcoal down from the mountains on their backs—that is, the women carry loads of charcoal. The men ride on donkeys. No mistaking the position of women in this society. I noticed a large percentage of these charcoal carriers had their noses eaten away by disease, but was not able to determine whether there is any occupational correlation. It seems more likely that they all come from the same heavily infected district.

Hashish is the drug of Islam, as alcohol is ours, opium the drug of the Far East, and cocaine that of South America. No effort is made to control its sale or use in Tangier, and every native café reeks of the smoke. They chop up the leaves on a wooden block, mix it with tobacco, and smoke it in little clay pipes with a long wooden stem.

Europeans occasion no surprise or overt resentment in Arab cafés. The usual drink is mint tea served very hot in a tall glass. If you hold the glass by top and bottom, avoiding the sides, it doesn't burn the hand. You can buy hashish, or *keif*, as they call it here, in any native café. It can also be purchased in sweet, resinous cakes to eat with hot tea. This resinous substance, a gum extracted from the cannabis plant, is the real hashish, and much more powerful than the leaves and flowers of the plant. The gum is called *majoun*, and the leaves *keif*. Good *majoun* is hard to find in Tangier.

Keif is identical with our marijuana, and we have here an opportunity to observe the effects of constant use on a whole population. I asked a European physician if he had noted any definite ill effects. He said: "In general, no. Occasionally there is drug psychosis, but it rarely reaches an acute stage where hospitalization is necessary." I asked if Arabs suffering from this psychosis are dangerous. He said: "I have never heard of any violence directly and definitely traceable to *keif*. To answer your question, they are usually not dangerous."

The typical Arab café is one room, a few tables and chairs, a huge copper or brass samovar for making tea and coffee. A raised platform covered with mats extends across one end of the room. Here the patrons loll about with their shoes off, smoking *keif* and playing cards. The game is Redondo, played with a pack of forty-two cards—rather an elementary card game. Fights start, stop, people walk around, play cards, smoke *keif,* all in a vast, timeless dream.

There is usually a radio turned on full volume. Arab music has neither beginning nor end. It is timeless. Heard for the first time, it may appear meaningless to a Westerner, because he is listening for a time structure that isn't there.

I talked with an American psychoanalyst who is practicing in Casablanca. He says you can never complete analysis with an Arab. Their superego structure is basically different. Perhaps you can't complete analysis with an Arab because he has no sense of time. He never completes anything. It is interesting that the drug of Islam is hashish, which affects the sense of time so that events, instead of appearing in an orderly structure of past, present and future, take on a simultaneous quality, the past and future contained in the present moment.

Tangier seems to exist on several dimensions. You are always finding streets, squares, parks you never saw before. Here fact merges into dream, and dreams erupt into the real world. Unfinished buildings fall into ruin and decay, Arabs move in silently like weeds and vines. A catatonic youth moves through the marketplace, bumping into people and stalls like a sleepwalker. A man, barefooted, in rags, his face eaten and tumescent with a horrible skin disease, begs with his eyes alone. He does not have the will left to hold out his hand. An old Arab passionately kisses the sidewalk. People stop to watch for a few moments with bestial curiosity, then move on.

Nobody in Tangier is exactly what he seems to be. Along with the bogus fugitives of the Socco Chico are genuine political exiles from Europe: Jewish refugees from Nazi Germany, Republican Spaniards, a selection of Vichy French and other collaborators, fugitive Nazis. The town is full of vaguely disreputable Europeans who do not have adequate documents to go anywhere else. So many people are here who cannot leave, lacking funds or papers or both. Tangier is a vast penal colony.

The special attraction of Tangier can be put in one word: exemption. Exemption from interference, legal or otherwise. Your private life is your own, to act exactly as you please. You will be talked about, of course. Tangier is a gossipy town, and everyone in the foreign colony knows everyone else. But that is all. No legal pressure or pressure of public opinion will curtail your behavior. The cop stands here with his hands behind his back, reduced to his basic function of keeping order. That is all he does. He is the other extreme from the thought police of police states, or our own vice squad.

Tangier is one of the few places left in the world where, so long as you don't proceed to robbery, violence, or some form of crude, antisocial behavior, you can do exactly what you want. It is a sanctuary of noninterference.

II.
LEE'S
JOURNALS

LEE'S JOURNALS

Lee's face, his whole person, seemed at first glance completely anonymous. He looked like an FBI man, like anybody. But the absence of trappings, of anything remotely picturesque or baroque, distinguished and delineated Lee, so that seen twice you would not forget him. Sometimes his face looked blurred, then it would come suddenly into focus, etched sharp and naked by the flashbulb of urgency. An electric distinction poured out of him, impregnated his shabby clothes, his steel-rimmed glasses, his dirty gray felt hat. These objects could be recognized anywhere as belonging to Lee.

His face had the look of a superimposed photo, reflecting a

fractured spirit that could never love man or woman with complete wholeness. Yet he was driven by an intense need to make his love real, to change fact. Usually he selected someone who could not reciprocate, so that he was able—cautiously, like one who tests uncertain ice, though in this case the danger was not that the ice give way but that it might hold his weight—to shift the burden of not loving, of being unable to love, onto the partner.

The objects of his high-tension love felt compelled to declare neutrality, feeling themselves surrounded by a struggle of dark purposes, not in direct danger, only liable to be caught in the line of fire. Lee never came on with a kill-lover-and-self routine. Basically the loved one was always and forever an Outsider, a Bystander, an Audience.

Went to Brion Gysin's place in the Medina for lunch: Brion, Dave Morton, Leif and Marv, and a handsome New Zealander who is passing through the Zone. A ghastly, meaningless aggregate.

Morton said to me: "How long were you in medical school before they found out you weren't a corpse?"

The standard double entendres and coy references to test the stranger. Brion says: "I'm queer for shoes," and begins polishing his shoes during lunch.

Marv says: "I'm very sensitive to that word. I wish you wouldn't use it," rolling his round gray eyes, speckled with flaws and opaque spots like damaged marbles, at the young stranger. . . . Oh God!

But none of this is the real horror. Looking around the room, I suddenly saw that the other people were figures in a waking nightmare where no contact with anyone else is possible.

Somehow it was worse than a gathering of out-and-out squares, say the St. Louis country club set I was brought up with. There, a dreary formalism reigns. It is just dull. But this was horrible, pointing to some final impasse of communication. There was nothing said that needed to be said. The dry hum of negation and decay filled the room with its blighting frequency, a sound like insect wings rubbing together.

Dream: I am in Interzone some years ago. I meet a silly fairy who twists every remark into obscene, queer double entendre. Under this vacuous camping I see pure evil. We meet two lesbians, and they say, "Hello, boys," a dead, ritual greeting from which I turn away in disgust. The fairy follows me, moves into a house with me. I feel nauseated, as if a loathsome insect had attached itself to my body.

I am walking out along a dry, white road on the outskirts of town. There is danger here. A dry, brown, vibrating hum or frequency in the air, like insect wings rubbing together. I pass a village: mounds about two feet high, of black cloth over wire frames like a vast hive.

Back in the city. Everywhere is the dry hum. Not a sound, exactly, but a frequency, a wavelength. A Holy Man with a black face is causing the waves. He operates from a tower-like structure covered with cloth.

I contract to assassinate the Holy Man. An Arab gives me a pink slip to present at a gun store, where a rifle with a telescopic sight will be issued to me. A Friend walks with me. He says: "There is no use to oppose the Holy Man. The Holy Man is reality. The Holy Man is Right."

"You're wrong," I say. "Wrong! I don't want to see you again for all eternity."

I hide from the Friend in a florist's shop, under a case of flowers. He stands by the case as though at my coffin, crying and wringing his hands and begging me to give up the assassination of the Holy Man. I am crying too, my tears falling in yellow dust, but I won't give up.

It is frequently said that the Great Powers will never give up the Interzone because of its value as a listening post. It is in fact the listening post of the world, the slowing pulse of a decayed civilization, that only war can quicken. Here East meets West in a final debacle of misunderstanding, each seeking the Answer, the Secret, from the other and not finding it, because neither has the Answer to give.

I catch sluggish flies in the air with the curious pleasure one derives from taking an eyelash from an eye, or extracting a hair from a nostril, the moment when the hair gives way with a little snap and you turn the greasy black hair between finger and thumb, looking at the white root, reluctant to let it go. So I felt the cold fly moving between my fingers, and the soft crunch as I delicately crushed the head to avoid a hemorrhage of sticky juice or blood— Where does the blood come from? Do they bite and suck blood?— finally letting the dead fly drop to the floor, spinning like a dry leaf.

Failure is mystery. A man does not mesh somehow with time-place. He has savvy, the ability to interpret the data collected by technicians, but he moves through the world like a ghost, never able to find the time-place and person to put anything into effect, to give it flesh in a three-dimensional world.

I could have been a successful bank robber, gangster, business executive, psychoanalyst, drug trafficker, explorer, bullfighter, but the conjuncture of circumstances was never there. Over the years I begin to doubt if my time will ever come. It will come, or it will not come. There is no use trying to force it. Attempts to break through have led to curbs, near disasters, warnings. I cultivate an alert passivity, as though watching an opponent for the slightest sign of weakness.

Of course there is always the possibility of reckless break-through, carrying a pistol around and shooting anybody who annoys me, taking narcotic supplies at gunpoint, *amok* a form of active suicide. Even that would require some signal from outside, or from so deep inside that it comes to the same thing. I have always seen inside versus outside as a false dichotomy. There is no sharp line of separation. Perhaps:

"Give it to me straight, Doc."

"Very well . . . A year perhaps, following a regime . . ." He is reaching for a pad.

"Never mind the regime. That's all I wanted to know."

Or simply the explosion of knowing, finally: "This is your last chance to step free of the cautious, aging, frightened flesh. What are you waiting for? To die in an old men's home, draping your fragile buttocks on a bench in the dayroom?"

Just thought of the story about how cats sit on your chest and breathe your breath out of you so you suffocate. Just sit there, you dig, their nose one-quarter inch from yours, and whenever you take a breath you get the cat's exhaust carbon dioxide. This story is like the Protocols of the Elders of Zion. Invented by cat-haters. So I start an anti-cat movement, pointing out their sneaky, sensual, unmoral traits, and begin wholesale extermination, genocide of the feline concept. There is always money in hate.

Perhaps Hitler was right in a way. That is, perhaps certain subspecies of genus *Homo sapiens* are incompatible. Live and let live is impossible. If you let live, they will kill you by creating an environment in which you have no place and will die out. The present psychic environment is increasingly difficult for me to endure, but there is still leeway, slack that could be taken up at any time. Safety lies in exterminating the type that produces the environment in which you cannot live. So I will die soon—why bother? Some form of transmigration seems to me probable. I am now, therefore I always was and always will be.

Looking down at my shiny, dirty trousers that haven't been changed in months, the days gliding by, strung on a syringe with a long thread of blood . . . it is easy to forget sex and drink and all the sharp pleasures of the body in this Limbo of negative pleasure, this thick cocoon of comfort.

More and more trouble at the *farmacía*. Spent all day until 5 P.M. to score two boxes of Eukodal. I'm running out of everything now. Out of veins, out of money. I can sense the static at the drugstore, the mutterings of control like a telephone off the hook.

"*Muy difícil ahora,*" the druggist tells me.

What is this creeping cancer of control? The suicided German is a plant, a pretext— Some days ago I was standing in a bar when a man touched my arm. I immediately made him for fuzz. In my pocket I had a box of methadone ampules I had just bought in the Plaza Farmacía. Could he be concerned about that? No, not in the Zone. He asked me if I was Max Gustav. I said, "No," naturally. The cop had a passport and showed me Gustav's picture, which he thought resembled me.

Next day I read in the paper that Max Gustav had been found dead in a ditch outside the town, apparently a suicide from overdose of Nembutal. It seems at the time the cop asked if I was Max they did not know he was dead. He had checked out of his hotel, leaving a suitcase. After two days the hotel called the law. They opened the suitcase, found the passport, and started looking for Max Gustav. . . . Well, the next time I went to the Plaza Farmacía they would not sell me methadone ampules without a script. A new regulation had gone into effect as a result of Max Gustav's suicide.

And that shows how things are related, or something. Bill Gains here would be the last straw. But everything has two faces. You need a paper now for everything. Why not apply for a permit to buy junk?

Such a sharp depression. I haven't felt like this since the day Joan died.

Spent the morning sick, waiting for Eukodal. Kept seeing familiar faces, people I had seen as store clerks, waiters, et cetera. In a small town these familiar faces accumulate and back up on you, so you are choked with familiarity on every side.

Sitting in front of the Interzone Café, sick, waiting for Eukodal. A boy walked by and I turned my head, following his loins the way a lizard turns its head, following the course of a fly.

Running short of money. Must kick habit.

What am I trying to do in writing? This novel is about transitions, larval forms, emergent telepathic faculty, attempts to control and stifle new forms.

I feel there is some hideous new force loose in the world like a creeping sickness, spreading, blighting. Remoter parts of the world seem better now, because they are less touched by it. Control, bureaucracy, regimentation, these are merely symptoms of a deeper sickness that no political or economic program can touch. What is the sickness itself?

Dream: Found a man with both hands cut off. I was pouring water on the stubs to stop the bleeding— Years ago in New York a young hoodlum borrowed a gun from me and never returned it. In a spasm of hate, I put a curse on him. A few days later both his hands were blown off when a gasoline drum exploded while he was working on it. He died. Are curses effective? Of course they are, to some extent.

More and more physical symptoms of depression. The latest is a burning sensation in the chest.

Until the age of thirty-five, when I wrote *Junky*, I had a special abhorrence for writing, for my thoughts and feelings put down on a piece of paper. Occasionally I would write a few sentences and then stop, overwhelmed with disgust and a sort of horror. At the present time, writing appears to me as an absolute necessity, and at the same time I have a feeling that my talent is lost and I can accomplish nothing, a feeling like the body's knowledge of disease, which the mind tries to evade and deny.

This feeling of horror is always with me now. I had the same feeling the day Joan died; and once when I was a child, I looked out into the hall, and such a feeling of fear and despair came over me, for no outward reason, that I burst into tears. I was looking into the future then. I recognize the feeling, and what I saw has not yet been realized. I can only wait for it to happen. Is it some ghastly occurrence like Joan's death, or simply deterioration and failure and final loneliness, a dead-end setup where there is no one I can contact? I am just a crazy old bore in a bar somewhere with my routines? I don't know, but I feel trapped and doomed.

Waiting for Eukodal, I was subject to a series of beggars. Two girls paralyzed from the waist down, swinging around on blocks. They bar the way, clutching at my pants legs. An English seaman on the beach. He gets his face very close to mine, and says, "You may be in the same position someday." I go into a café and sit at the counter drinking a cup of coffee. A child about seven years old, barefooted and dirty, touches my arm. These people are raised in beggary and buggery.

The nightmare feeling of my childhood is more and more my habitual condition. Is this a prevision of atomic debacle? Dream of a sixteenth-century Norwegian: He saw a black, mushroom-shaped cloud darkening the earth.

We have a new type of rule now. Not one-man rule, or rule of aristocracy or plutocracy, but of small groups elevated to positions of absolute power by random pressures, and subject to political and economic factors that leave little room for decision. They are representatives of abstract forces who have reached power through surrender of self. The iron-willed dictator is a thing of the past. There will be no more Stalins, no more Hitlers. The rulers of this most insecure of all worlds are rulers by accident, inept, frightened pilots at the controls of a vast machine they cannot understand, calling in experts to tell them which buttons to push.

Junk is a key, a prototype of life. If anyone fully understood junk, he would have some of the secrets of life, the final answers.

I have mentioned the increased sensitivity to dreamlike feelings of nostalgia that always accompany light junk sickness. This morning when I woke up without junk, I closed my eyes and saw cliffs on the outskirts of a town, with houses on top of them, and china-blue sky, and white linen snapping in a cold spring wind.

The pure pleasure of cold Whistle on a hot summer afternoon of my childhood. In the 1920s the United States, even the Midwest, was a place of glittering possibilities. You could be a gangster, a hard-drinking reporter, a jittery stockbroker, an expatriate, a successful writer. The possibilities spilled out in front of you like a rich display of merchandise. Sitting on the back steps drinking Whistle at twilight on a summer evening, hearing the streetcars clang past on Euclid Avenue, I felt the excitement and nostalgia of the twenties tingling in my groin.

Interesting that out of morphine has been made the perfect antidote for morphine, and that it creates its exact antidote in the body. And from junk sickness comes a heightened sensitivity to impressions and sensation on the level of dream, myth, symbol. On the penis there might be bits of flesh half-putrescent and half-larval, separating from the host and degenerating to less specific tissue, a sort of life jelly that will take root and grow anywhere.

Seemed to see West St. Louis, the moving headlights on Lindell Boulevard. Very vivid for a moment. I was in a study with soft lights, an apartment probably. Horrible feeling of desolation. Imagine being old, paralyzed or blind, and forced to accept the charity of some St. Louis relation. I continue writing, but publication is hopeless. The book market is saturated. It is all done now by staff writers and is as much a job as working in an advertising agency. Not even anyone I can read it to, so that when I know it is good I feel more sad because then the loneliness is sharper.

Would it be possible to write a novel based on the actual facts of Interzone or anyplace?

Marv and Mohamed—this "friendship," as Sam calls it:
"Once he brought me a dead sparrow."
Marv's grating, continual laugh, his angular, graceless movements. They could not be called clumsy. Quick, not fumbling, he moves in galvanized, pathic jerks, never sliding into fluid grace, or off the other edge into actual tic.
And Mohamed—sulky, stupid, whore to the bone. He is a favorite among the Arabs because of his chunky, fat ass. A fat ass is considered highly desirable by the Arabs. How Oriental and dull at the same time, like a carryover from camel trading.
So Marv says all the time: "I don't mind him going with Arabs,

you understand, but just don't let me catch him with another American or a European. Better not let me catch either of them. You have to fight for what you want in this world."

I wonder if Mohamed has any desires that are really his, that is, starting from inside out and seeking the projection of his desire? But they don't function that way. They are excited by situation, not by fantasy. This is partly due to the immediate availability of sex to the Arab, which is difficult for an American—accustomed to frustration, certainly to delay, expense, buildup—to realize. The Arab achieves immediate satisfaction because he is willing to accept homosexual contact.

As Marv puts it: "It's three in the morning, so Ali meets Ahmed and says to him: 'Do you want to?' That's the standard phrase. The whole deal takes five minutes." It's expected the one who makes the proposition should give something to the other. A few pesetas, some cigarettes. Anything. A matter of form. So perhaps an Arab has no type he is looking for, no specialized desires at all. Man or woman, it's all sex to him. Like eating. Something you do every day.

No one I really want to see here. So far as friendship goes, I can't live off the country. So few people I want to see anywhere. KiKi is ten minutes' perfunctory talk or sex, and I am completely unable most of the time on accounta the family jewels is in hock to the Chinaman. Must cut down or kick. The price is going up to where I can't pay. Since that fucking German had to come here and commit suicide, you have to buy a script every time. Why couldn't he have done it someplace else? Or some other way? Waited all day until eight at night for two boxes.

A novel that consists of the facts as I see and feel them. How can it have a beginning or an end? It just runs along for a while and then stops, like Arab music.

I can hear some Arabs singing in the next house. This music goes on and on, up and down. Why don't they get bored with it and shut up? It says nothing, goes nowhere. There is no lift in it, no emotion. Sounds like a chorus of boys singing out lottery numbers, or a tobacco auction. Apparently they are beating a tambourine, dancing and singing. Every now and then they reach a meaningless climax and everybody lets out shrill yipes. Then they stop for a while, presumably resting for another period of the same routine. Is it sad, happy, sinister, sweet? Does it express any deep human emotions? If so, I don't feel it.

I have wondered if it would be possible to find a note of music that would produce orgasm in the listener, that would reach into the spinal column and touch a long white nerve. Tension grows in the abdomen and breaks in long waves through the body, colonic undulations rising to a sudden crescendo. Arab music sounds like that. An orgasm produced mechanically without emotion, a twanging on the nerves, a beating on the viscera.

After a shot I went up to the Bagdad and met Leif and Marv. The manager is an unsuccessful artist named Algren. If he has a first name, I never heard it. Tall, broad-shouldered, handsome, with a cold, imperious manner. When I first came to Interzone he was exhibiting some of his paintings. Not distinguished work. Vistas of the Sahara, the best of them recalling the bare, haunted rock and desert of Dalí's dream landscapes. There is skill, he can draw but he has no real reason to do so. I found he was as niggardly in putting out in personal relation as in painting. I could make no contact with him. He lives with a young Arab painter, a phony primitive. As a fashionable restaurateur, Algren is superb, just the correct frequency of glacial geniality. He expects the joint to become world-famous.

"Last night the coatroom was stacked with mink. There's a lot of money in Interzone," he says. Maybe, but it is a bit out of the way. A rich old woman put up the loot. Algren doesn't have dime one, but he's a character who will get rich by acting like he is rich already. And Algren is crazy in a way that will help. He has a paranoid conceit. He is a man who never has one good word to say for anybody, and that's the way a man should be to run a fashionable night spot. Everyone will want to be the exception, the one person he really likes.

He has some Arab musicians from the Rif, a three-man combo, and a little boy who dances and sings. The kid is about fourteen and small for his age, like all Arabs. There is no stir of adolescence in his face, no ferment, nothing there to awaken. The face of an old child, doll-like with a monkey's acquisitiveness. He puts the money you give him in his turban so it hangs down on his forehead. What does he do with the money? His voice is very loud, the up and down of Arab music bellowed out by this grasping, whirling doll. He twitches his hips not only sideways but up and over in a peculiar, double-jointed movement. His sexual and acquisitive drives are completely merged. It would never occur to him to go to bed with anyone for a reason other than money. There is about him a complete lack of youngness, of all the sweetness and un-certainty and shyness of youth. He is hard and brassy as an old whore, and to me about as interesting as a sexual object.

There is a nightmare feeling in Interzone with its glut of nylon shirts, cameras, watches, sex and opiates sold across the counter. Something profoundly menacing in complete laissez-faire. And the new police chief up there on the Hill, accumulating dossiers—I suspect him of unspeakable fetishistic practices with his files.

When the druggist sells me my daily ration of Eukodal, he smirks like I have picked up the bait to a trap. The whole Zone is a trap, and someday it will close. Not snap shut, but close slowly. We will see it closing, but there will be no escape, no place to go.

Speaking of the new chief of police reminds me, when I first got here KiKi's mother beefed about me to the fuzz I was debauching her only child, or so the story went. I was living in Matty's place, and Matty swore it was true, and claimed there was a detective prowling around outside the door—it turned out he wasn't a detective at all but an old queen who had his eye on KiKi, and the whole story was just Interzone bullshit. At the same time Antonio, the mooching Portuguese, starts a rumor there is junk heat on me. He hopes I will lam out of the Zone.

Matty is a pimp who loves his work, a fat, middle-aged, queer Cupid. He kept casting reproachful glances at me in the hall: "*Ach,* fifteen years in the Zone, and never before do I have such a thing in my house. Now is here since two weeks an English gentleman. With him I could make good business except my house is so watched at."

Bedroom farce of police and terrible mother coming in the front door. I try to push KiKi into Marv's room and he says: "Dump your hot kids someplace else, Lee." A handkerchief with come on it is extremely damning evidence. The best thing is to swallow it.

I am writing this in a hospital where I am taking the cure again. A typical Interzone setup. Jewish hospital, Spanish-run, with Catholic sisters as nurses. Like everything Spanish it is run in a sloppy, lackadaisical manner, thank God! No nurse walking in at the crack of dawn to slop tepid water all over you. No good explaining to some Swedish nurse from North Dakota how a junky can't stand the feel of water on his skin. I been here ten days and haven't had a bath. It is 8 A.M. and the day shift comes on sometime in the next half hour. In the room next to me someone is groaning. A horrible, inhuman sound, pushed out from the stomach. Why don't they give him a shot and shut him up? It's a drag. I hate to hear people groan, not because of pity but because it is a very irritating sound.

That reminds me of a skit I once wrote about a junky whose mother was dying of cancer, and he takes her morphine, substituting codeine. To substitute codeine was worse than stealing the morphine outright and substituting milk-sugar placebo. A placebo, by the shock, the gap between the pain-torn tissues straining for the relief of morphine, and the sheer nothingness in the placebo, might galvanize the body into a miracle, an immaculate fix. But codeine would blunt the edge of pain so that it would liquefy and spread, filling the cells like a gray fog, solid, impossible to dislodge.

"Better now?" The groaning had stopped.

"Much better, thank you," she said dryly.

She knows, he thought. *I could never fool her.*

Perhaps one would feel better in an out-and-out police state like Russia or satellite countries. The worst has happened. The outer world realizes your deepest fears—or desires? You don't get bends of the spirit from sudden changes of pressure. Inner and outer pressure are equalized.

So I wrote a story about a man who gets the wrong passport in a Turkish bath in the Russian Zone of Vienna, and he can't get back through the Iron Curtain. Incomplete, of course. What you think I am, a hack?

The sky over Vienna was a light, hard, china blue, and a cold spring wind whipped Martin's loose gabardine topcoat around his thin body. He felt the ache of desire in his loins, like a toothache when the pain is light and different from any other pain. He turned a corner; the Danube stabbed his eyes with a thousand points of light, and he felt the full force of the wind and had to lean forward to maintain balance.

If there's no guard at the line there can't be too much danger, he thought. *They could hardly accuse me of spying in a Turkish bath.* He saw a café and went in. A huge room, almost empty. Green upholstered seats like old Pullman cars. A sullen waiter with a round pimply face and white eyelashes took his order for a double brandy. He swallowed the brandy straight. For a moment he gagged, then his stomach smoothed out in waves of warmth and euphoria. He ordered another brandy. The waiter was smiling now.

What the hell, he thought. *All they could do is kick me out of the Russian Zone.*

He sat back anticipating the warm embrace of steam, letting go, liquefying like an amoeba, dissolving in warmth and comfort and desire.

Why draw the line anywhere? What a man wants to do he will do sooner or later, in thought or in fact. . . . But nobody is giving you an argument. The third brandy was anesthetizing the centers of caution. *I'm hard up and I want a boy, and I'm going to the Roman Baths, Russian Zone or no. Too bad we didn't have a queer representative when they split up Vienna. We'd have gone to the barricades before Russia got the Roman Baths.*

He saw a legion of embattled queens behind a barricade of Swedish-modern furniture. They staggered and died with great histrionic gestures and pathic screams. They were all tall, thin, ungainly queens in Levi's and lumberjack shirts, with long yellow hair and insane blue eyes, all screaming, screaming. He shuddered. *Perhaps I'd better just go back to the hotel and . . . no, by God!*

The streetcar was crowded and he had to stand. The people looked gray, hostile, suspicious, avoiding his glance. They were passing the Prater. He was in the Russian Zone. He remembered the Prater before the war, a huge park always full of people and plenty of pickups. Now it was an expanse of rubble with one vast Ferris wheel, bleak and menacing against the cold blue sky. He got off the streetcar. The conductor stood leaning out of the back platform watching Martin until the streetcar turned the corner. Martin pretended to look for a cigarette.

Yes, there were the Roman Baths, looking much the same. The street was empty. Perhaps there would be no boys. But a youth sidled up to him and asked for a light. *Not too good,* he decided. *I'll find better inside.*

He paid for a room, leaving his wallet and passport in a deposit box.

(This is after he has got the wrong passport, been arrested and deported to Budapest, or somewhere far behind the Iron Curtain.)

He learned a new kind of freedom, the freedom of living in continual tension and fear to the limit of his inner fear and tension so the pressure was at least equalized, and for the first time in his adult life he knew the meaning of complete relaxation, complete pleasure in the moment. He felt alive with his whole being. The forces that were intended to crush his dignity and existence as an individual delineated him so that he had never felt surer of his own worth and dignity.

And he was not alone. Slowly he discovered a vast, dreamlike underground: a cop examining his papers would suddenly turn into a friend. And he learned the meaning of the hostile, averted faces on the streetcar in Vienna, learned to distrust the friendship too quickly offered.

Martin had lost fifteen pounds since leaving the West. His hand rested now on his stomach, feeling the muscle hard and alive with an animal alertness. Steps on the stairs. Two men, strangers. He knew the step of everyone in the One World pension. He slid off the bed. Moving with economy and precision, he shoved a heavy wardrobe in front of the door. He crossed the room, opened the window and stepped out onto the fire escape, closing the window behind him. He climbed a shaky iron ladder to the roof. He heard the wardrobe crash to the floor. Seven feet to the next roof. He looked around. No plank, nothing. He heard the window open. *I'll have to jump*, he decided.

(To be continued)

Went to bed with KiKi. He said he couldn't come because he is all wore out from wet dreams about me the night before. That really takes the rag offen the bush.

Developed routine during dinner with Kells Elvins. We kidnap the Sacred Black Stone out of Mecca and hold it for ransom. We swoop down in a helicopter, throw the Stone in and take off with it like a great roc, the Arabs following the 'copter across the square, reaching up at it and shouting imprecations. (Maybe the Stone is too big to move?)

Lee sat with the syringe poised in his left hand, pondering the mystery of blood. Certain veins he could hit at two-thirty in the afternoon. Others were night veins, veins that appeared and disappeared at random. Lee found his hunches were seldom wrong. If he reached for the syringe with his right hand, it meant try the left arm. His body knew what vein could be hit. He let the body take over, as in automatic writing, when he was preparing to pick up.

There was a single candle burning in a brass stick on the bed table. KiKi and Lee lay side by side in bed, a sheet thrown across their bodies waist high. They passed a *keif* cigarette back and forth, inhaling deeply and holding the inhale. KiKi had a case of benign shingles, and there was a great hive on his back and swelling in the glands under his arms. Lee ran gentle fingers over the inflamed area, asked questions, nodded gravely from time to time. The candle light and smoke, the low voices, imparted a quality of ritual to the scene. . . .

Following is a story of a young man in Spain sentenced to be hanged by a council of war (the military handles capital cases in Spain):

Antonio sat down on the iron shelf covered with old newspapers that was his bed. He lay down on his side and pulled his knees up to his chest, hands pressed against his genitals.

A council of war! he thought. *That completes the picture of a barbarous, obscene ritual like an Indian tribe's. They've been trying to get me like this ever since they found out I'd been born alive. But I had an animal's feel for traps—until they found the right bait. It was a clumsy snare, and I could have seen the noose under the leaves that first night in Tío Pepe's. That is, I could have seen it if I hadn't been looking someplace else. . . .*

Fade out . . . Flash back . . . Music (obviously I have an eye on TV and Hollywood):

It was early for Tío Pepe's, which is a late place that gets going when the bars close down, after one o'clock. No one at the bar. I ordered a cognac. There was a boy standing in front of the jukebox. He had on one of those summer shirts with holes in it, a white shirt hanging outside his pants. Through the shirt, in a halo of hideous man-made colors, chlorophyll greens, reds and oranges of synthetic soft drinks, the purples of a fluorescent-lighted cocktail lounge, the ghastly light pinks and blues of religious objects, I could see the lean young body alive with an animal alertness. He was leaning against the jukebox, his hip thrown to one side, his face bent over, reading the song titles, all the awkwardness and grace and sweetness of adolescence in his stance, those terrible colors playing over him.

He looks like an advertisement for something, I thought, but that wasn't exactly what I meant. There was some significance in the young figure leaning over the jukebox that eluded me. Then he turned around, pivoting with a sudden movement. I could hear my own breath suck in with a sharp hiss of air. He didn't have any face. It was a mass of scar tissue. . . .

I see the way to solve contradictions, to unite fragmentary, unconnected projects: I will simply transcribe Lee's impressions of Interzone. The fragmentary quality of the work is inherent in the method and will resolve itself so far as necessary. That is, I include the author, Lee, in the novel, and by so doing separate myself from him so that he becomes another character, central to be sure, occupying a special position, but not myself at all. This could go on in an endless serial arrangement, but I would always be the observer and not the participant by the very act of writing about a figure who represents myself.

I feel guilty writing this when I should be up to my balls in work. But feller say: "Nothing is lost." . . . A horrible vision of suffocating under the accumulated piss and shit and nail clippings and eyelashes and snot excreted by my soul and body, backing up like atomic waste. "Go get lost for Chrissakes!" I already made a novel outa letters. I can always tuck one in somewhere, bung up a hole with it, you know. . . .

I hear that baneful, unfrocked Lt. Commander prowling about the halls. They took his buttons off and cut his stripes away, but unfortunately neglected to hang him in the morning or at any other time. The reference, in case you are fortunate enough not to know, is to "The Hanging of Danny Deever" by Kipling. For a real bum kick you should hear a decaying, corseted tenor singing "The Hanging of Danny Deever," followed by "Trees" as an unsolicited encore.

Like I say, this fucking ex-Commander is casting a spell of silliness over me so that I sometimes come up with these awful, queer double entendres myself. Last night I told him straight, by God I wasn't going to stand still for any more of his shit: "Don't you know about Joe Reeves? Why, I hear he likes boys! Did you ever hear of such a thing, Bill? Heh heh heh." Rolling his eyes at Kells.

So I really had all I could take. And the typewriter is fucked again. I'm a martyr to this fucking typewriter—a man as basically unmechanical as I am should never buy used machinery—but before I'll ask help from that Commander I'll write with blood and a hypodermic needle.

Loaded on methadone. I bought out Interzone and the south end of Spain on Eukodal. Like I say, loaded, impotent, convulsed with disembodied limitless desire. Appointment with KiKi *mañana*. I am supposed to be taking the cure again. KiKi has my clothes and money and is doling out ampules—

I pulled a sneak. Pants borrowed off a clothesline, *dégagé* in a dirty sweatshirt like returning from tennis or a hike on the mountain, finally managed to cash one of my special traveler's checks. Even my traveler's checks are wrong, vaguely disreputable and disturbing. No one thinks they are actually forged or counterfeit, you understand. They just feel something wrong with me.

A fat blond beast of a desk sergeant throwing himself at the feet of a thin, crippled, red-haired lush worker: sparse red hair, the junky gray felt hat which leaves a line on his forehead when he takes it off—it is that tight. So this cop comes down from the rostrum of his desk and grovels at the feet of this skinny little middle-aged lush worker known as Red from Brooklyn, to distinguish him from another Red, who has no such definite and particularizing place of residence. Red shrinks back, expecting to get worked over.

"Red!" A horrible sound of defeat, a sordid battle fought and lost in a psyche as bleak as a precinct cell. "Reddie Boy!" He makes a kissing bite for Red's shoe. Red retreats again.

"Now, Lieutenant! I didn't so much as put my hand out."

The sergeant jumps up like a great albino toad. He reaches out and grabs the trembling lush worker by the coat lapels.

"Lieutenant! Listen to me. I didn't."

"Reddie Boy!" He throws his fat but powerful arms around Red, pinioning both of Red's arms. He runs one hand up behind Red's neck, kisses him brutally, repeatedly.

"Reddie Boy! How I've wanted you all these years! I remember the first time you came in, with Dolan from the Fifteenth. Only it wasn't the Fifteenth then, it was the Ninth. . . ."

Red gives a horrible, sickly, cautious smile. *The fuzz has flipped. I gotta play it cool . . . cool. . . .*

"Many's the night I've cried for you like this, Reddie Boy."

"Jeez, not that way, Sarge. I got piles."

"You haven't been a naughty boy with someone else, have you? Wonder if we could use this floor wax?" This last sentence in his hard, practical cop voice.

Someone just died in the hospital downstairs. I can hear them chanting something, and women crying. It's the old Jew who was annoying me with his groans. . . . Well, get this stiff outa here. It's a bringdown for the other patients. This isn't a funeral parlor.

What levels and time shifts involved in transcribing these notes: reconstruction of the past, the immediate present—which conditions selection of the material—the emergent future, all hitting me at once, sitting here junk-sick because I got some cut ampules of methadone last night and this morning.

I just went down to the head and passed the dead man's room. Sheet pulled up over his face, two women sniffling. I saw him several times, in fact this morning an hour before he died. An ugly little man with a potbelly and scraggly, dirty beard, always groaning. How bleak and sordid and meaningless his death!

God grant I never die in a fucking hospital! Let me die in some *louche* bistro, a knife in my liver, my skull split with a beer bottle, a pistol bullet through the spine, my head in spit and blood and beer, or half in the urinal so the last thing I know is the sharp ammonia odor of piss— I recall in Peru a drunk passed out in the urinal. He lay there on the floor, his hair soaked with piss. The urinal leaked, like all South American pissoirs, and there was half an inch of piss on the floor— Or let me die in an Indian hut, on a sandbank, in jail, or alone in a furnished room, on the ground someplace or in an alley, on street or subway platform, in a wrecked car or plane, my steaming guts splattered over torn pieces of metal. . . . Anyplace, but not in a hospital, not in bed . . .

This is really a prayer. "If you have prayed, the thing may chance." Certainly I would be atypical of my generation if I didn't die with my boots on. Dave Kammerer stabbed by his boy with a scout knife, Tiger Terry killed by an African lion in a border-town nightclub, Joan Burroughs shot in the forehead by a drunken idiot—myself—doing a William Tell, trying to shoot a highball glass off her head, Cannastra killed climbing out of a moving subway for one more drink— His last words were "Pull me back!" His friends tried to pull him back inside, but his coat ripped in their hands and then he hit a post—Marvie dead from an overdose of horse—

I see Marvie in a cheap furnished room on Jane Street, where I used to serve him—sounds kinda dirty, don't it?—I mean sell him caps of H, figuring it was better to deliver to his room than meet him someplace, he is such a ratty-looking citizen, with his black shoes and no socks in December. Once I delivered him his cap, and he tied up. I was looking out the window—it is nerveracking to watch someone look for a vein. When I turned around he had passed out, and the blood had run back into the dropper, it was hanging onto his arm full of blood, like a glass leech— So I see him there on the bed in a furnished room, slowly turning blue around the lips, the dropper full of blood clinging to his arm. Outside it is getting dark. A neon sign flashes off and on, off and on, each flash picking out his face in a hideous red-purple glow— "Use Gimpie's H. It's the greatest!" Marvie won't have to hustle tomorrow. He has scored for the Big Fix.

—Leif the Dane drowned with all hands in the North Sea—he was a drag anyhoo. Roy went wrong and hanged himself in the Tombs—he always used to say: "I don't see how a pigeon can live with himself." And P. Holt, the closest friend of my childhood, cut his jugular vein on a broken windshield . . . dead before they got him out of the car. A few of them died in hospitals or first-aid stations, but they had already had it someplace else. Foster, one of my anthropology friends in Mexico, died of bulbar polio. "He was dead when he walked in the door," the doctor at the hospital said later. "I felt like telling him, 'Why don't you check straight into a funeral parlor, pick your coffin and climb into it? You've got just about time.' "

I've had trouble with this Spanish methadone before. Often I have bought boxes with one or two empty ampules. Accident? Spanish sloppiness? Ixnay. These Spanish factories are flooding Southern Europe with methadone.

Is it safer to put an empty ampule in every ten boxes or so, or to fill all the ampules with adulterated mixture? Hard to say. People are more likely to beef about empties, but it is easier to alibi. Accidents can happen—though they shouldn't happen in a methadone factory. Not that kind of accident. A beef is less likely with an adulterated mixture, but more serious if it occurs, and somebody who hasn't been paid off, or who has a political angle, starts making spot analyses of the product. There is no alibi-ing that. And they are getting too greedy. Last night's shot was *plain water*. That's not smart.

The Man is getting edgy. His boy is squawking for a star sapphire: "Daddy, you wanna get the best for me." His blonde wants a custom-made Daimler so long it can't turn corners—only also-rans turn corners. If you got real class to you, you never look sideways. The bang-tails are running offbeat, some citizen unloaded a salted uranium mine on him. (The uranium mine is a new con. You plant a tube of atomic waste in the mine site so the Geiger counter goes wild over it. Or you can use a gimmicked Geiger counter with an electric motor concealed in it so you can speed it up or slow it down.)

My thoughts have been turning to crime lately. And of all crimes, blackmail seems to me the most artistically satisfying. I mean, the Moment of Truth when you see all his bluff and bluster and front collapse, when you know you've got him. His next words—when he can talk—will be: "How much do you want?" That must be real tasty. A man could get his rocks off on a deal like that.

Like a guy pushed his boy off a balcony and claimed it was an accident, the kid slipped on a gob of K-Y and catapulted over the rail. No witnesses. He seems to be in the clear. Then Willy Lee drops around.

Lee: "You see, Mr. Throckmorton, I'm broke."

Throckmorton: "Broke! I don't know why you come to me with this revolting disclosure. It's extremely distasteful. Have you no pride?"

Lee: "I thought you might want to help a fellow American, and buy this gadget off me." He shows a German spy camera attached to powerful field glasses for long-range pictures. "It's worth quite a bit."

Throckmorton: "Take it to a pawnshop. I have no interest in photography."

Lee: "But this is a very special gadget. Look from that balcony. . . . *Say*, isn't that the balcony that kid fell from?"

Throckmorton looks at him coldly. Lee stammers, pretends to be embarrassed.

Lee: "Now I hope I haven't gone and said the wrong thing. Must have been a terrible shock for you, losing a friend . . . and such a *good* friend. . . . What I wanted to say was from that balcony you can hardly see my trap over on the wrong side of the Medina, but if I took a picture from that balcony it would show my place and how dirty the windows are and how one has a broken pane mended with adhesive tape. . . ."

Throckmorton (looking at his watch): "I'm not interested. Now if you will excuse me, I have an appointment. . . ."

Lee: "I'm sorry to take up your time like this. . . . Like I was saying, you could take a picture that would show my place, or you could take a picture in the other direction—one that would show *your* place. I've taken some pictures of your place, Mr. Throckmorton. . . . I hope you won't think me presumptuous." He pulls out some photos. "I'm a pretty good photographer. Maybe you would want to buy some of these pictures I took of your house and that balcony. . . ."

Throckmorton: "Will you please leave my house."

Lee: "But, Mr. Throckmorton, one of these pictures is really interesting." He holds the picture three inches in front of Throckmorton's face. Throckmorton starts back. A cry of anger dies away to a gurgle in his throat. He reaches for a chair and collapses into it, like an old man having a stroke.

Lee: "Like the song say, *Mister* Throckmorton, you're beginning to see the light. . . . What's your first name, lover?" He sits on the arm of Throckmorton's chair and playfully ruffles his hair. "I got like a presentiment we're going to get to know each other real well . . . see quite a bit of each other."

—

I have a feeling that my real work I can't or, on a deep level, won't begin. What I do is only evasion, sidetrack, notes. I am walking around the shores of a lake, afraid to jump in, but pretending to study the flora and fauna—those two old bags. I must put myself, every fucking cell of me, at the disposal of this work.

Oh, God! Sounds like posthumous biographical material—Lee's letters to his beloved friend and agent, who writes back that the work must develop in its own way and reveal as much of itself to me as I am able to interpret and transcribe. I have but to act with straightaheadedness, without fear or holding back.

"At this time the creative energies of Lee were at lowest ebb. He was subject to acute depressions. 'At times,' he writes in a letter to his agent, 'my breath comes in gasps,' or again, 'I have to remember to breathe.' "

But the fragmentary, unconnected quality of my work is inherent in the method, and will resolve itself as far as is necessary. The Tangier novel will consist of Lee's impressions of Tangier, instead of the outworn novelistic pretense that he is dealing directly with his characters and situations. That is, *I include the author in the novel*.

Civilian casualties of those books on combat judo and guerrilla war. Country club cocktail party: A man who had been a great athlete in his youth, still powerful but fattish, a sullen-faced ash blond with droopy lips, stands in front of another man, looking at him with stupid belligerence.

"Bovard, I could kill you in thirty seconds. No, in ten seconds. I have a book on combat judo. . . . Like this—" He leaps on Bovard, planting a knee in his back. "I hook my left middle finger into your right eye, meanwhile my knee is in your kidney and I am crushing your Adam's apple with my right elbow and reaching around to stamp on your instep with . . ."

Sharp words with the *criada*. Half an hour past breakfast time, I ring and ask for breakfast and the silly little bitch comes on sulky and surprised, like I was out of line.

I say sharply: "Look, *señorita*" (there is no English equivalent for *señorita*, which means a young, well-brought-up, unbanged young lady, I mean a virgin; you even call sixty-year-old whores *señorita* as a politeness—especially if you want something from them, you dig, I shouldn't take it upon myself to imply she *isn't* *señorita*)—so I say, "Look, *señorita*, breakfast is at eight. It's now eight-thirty."

I am not one of those weak-spirited, sappy Americans who want to be liked by all the people around them. I don't care if people hate my guts; I assume most of them do. The important question is what are they in a position to do about it. My affections, being concentrated on a few people, are not spread all over Hell in a vile attempt to placate sulky, worthless shits.

Of course, they could cut off my junk. That happened once and I beefed loud, long and high up, straight to the head croaker of this crummy trap. (I'm about the only cash customer they got. If I'd claimed to be half-Jewish I would be here for free.) My purpose in beefing was just in case somebody on the premises lifted the ampule and give me a shot of water, though the stuff was probably cut at the factory like Jewish babies, like all babies now. There is a night nurse who looks like junk, but it's hard for me to be sure with women and Chinese. Anyhoo, she give me a shot of water one night and I don't want her ministering to me no more—

Actually I savor like old brandy, rolling it on my tongue, the impotent hate of people who cannot, dare not retaliate. *That is, you dig, if I am in the right putting them down,* if they really have come up lousy. My epitaph on Old Dave the Pusher who died last year in Mexico, D.F.: "He looks like junk as he would catch another user in his strong toils of grace."

This place is *mad.* There are six people in my room now, washing the floor, putting up a mirror, taking the bed out and putting another one in, hanging curtains, fixing the light switch, all falling over each other and yelling in Spanish and Arabic, and the piss-elegant electrician only deigns to speak French—in Interzone it is a sign of class to speak nothing but French. You ask a question in Spanish, they answer in French, which is supposed to put you in your place. Citizens who come on with the "I only speak French" routine are the sorriest shits in the Zone, all pretentious, genteel—with the ghastly English connotation of lower-middle-class phony elegance—and generally don't have franc one. This electrician looks like a walking character armor with nothing inside it. I can see some Reichian analyst who has succeeded in dislodging the electrician's character armor. The analyst staggers back, blasted, blighted, a trembling hand covers his eyes: "Put it back! For the love of Christ, put it back!"

I met Mark Bradford, the playwright. He says: "I didn't catch your name."

"William Lee."

"Oh!" He drops my hand. "Well . . . uh, excuse me." He left Interzone the following day.

To a person in the medium of success, Willy Lee is an ominous figure. You meet him on the way down. He never hits a place when it is booming. When Willy Lee shows, the desert wind is blowing dust into empty bars and hotels, jungle vines are covering the oil derricks. A mad realtor sits in a spectral office, a famished jackal gnaws his numb, gangrenous foot: "Yes sir," he says, "this development is building right up."

A successful composer says to his protégé, a young Arab poet:

"Start packing, Titmouse. I just saw Willy Lee in the Socco Chico. Interzone has had it."

"Why, is he dangerous? You don't have to see him."

"*See* him—I should think not. It's like this: A culture gets its special stamp—Mayan, Northwest Coast, North Pacific—probably from one person or small group of people, who originally exuded these archetypes. After that, the archetypes are accepted unchanged for thousands of years. Well, Lee goes around exuding his own archetypes. It isn't done anymore. Already the Interzone Café reeks of rotting, aborted, larval archetypes. You notice that vibrating soundless hum in the Socco? That means someone is making archetypes in the area and you'd best evacuate right now. . . . Look, I am a success because I mesh with existing archetypes. If I accept, or even get to know, Lee's archetypes . . . and his routines!!!" The composer shudders. "Not me. Get packing, we're meeting Cole in Capri."

I just lit up. . . . A very dangerous party, Miss Green. Just one long drag on the unnatural teat she's got under her left arm and you are stoned, Pops. . . . In Mexico once I picked up on some bum-kick weed, and then got on a bus. I had a small pistol, a .41-caliber double-barreled Remington derringer in a holster tucked inside my belt so it was pointing just where the leg joins the body. . . . Suddenly I could feel the gun go off, smell the powder smoke, the singed cloth, feel the horrible numb shock, then the pit-pat of blood dripping like piss on the floor. . . . Later I examined the gun and found the safety half-cock was broken and such accidental discharge was quite possible.

I see the Un-American Committee has got around to Chris Goodwin. About time. I knew him when, dearie. A rank card-carrying

Scumunist. Queer, of course. He married a transvestite Jew Liz who worked on *Sundial,* that left-wing tabloid. —You recall the rag folded when their angel, an Albanian condom tycoon who came on like an English gentleman—the famous Merchant of Sex, who scandalized the International Set when he appeared at the Duc du Ventre's costume ball as a walking prick covered by a huge condom—went broke and shot himself during World War II. He couldn't get rubber, and Alcibiades Linton, the Houston Bubble Gum King, beat him out on Mexican chicle—perhaps these long parentheses should be relegated to footnotes. —I don't know why Chris married her. Probably for the looks of the thing, not knowing exactly how such things do look. . . . Did I ever tell you about my *New Yorker* cartoon? One State Department pansy visiting another. Kids crawling all over both of them, so the visiting swish says to the other: "Really, my dear, this front thing can be carried too far." —Anyhoo, his Liz wife was killed by Kurds in Pakistan—the reference is not to sour milk but to a species of Himalayan bandit. So Chris comes back with his dead wife in a jeep and says: "Poor Rachel. She was the life of every party. Kurds, you know." Kurds indeed. He liquidated her on orders from Moscow. Fact is, she "had taken to living on a slope of aristocracy," and ultimately "became crude and rampant"—I quote from the Moscow Ultimatum. I am leaving a reference to Turds for Milton Berle or anyone else who wants it. . . .

Also an improvement on the new anti-enzyme toothpaste to keep off lieutenants j.g. (junior grade) . . . a queen-repellent smelling of decayed queen flesh. (Shark repellent issued by the Navy smells like decayed sharks. Will put even a shark off his feed.)

The unfrocked commander lost his breevies, as he calls them, his jockstrap bathing suit that just does cover his equipment. That is, the maid lost his breevies in the laundry and he has been arguing with her about it for the past week.

Today the maid showed me the breevies and said: "Are they

his?" pointing to his room, and I said: "I presume that they are . . . they certainly aren't yours, madam."

Typical Interzone conversation: "My dear, let me tell you where you can buy the most marvelous cakes. Doughnut dough outside, hot custard filling, and rolled in sugar . . . Just opposite the Mecca bus terminal in the wholesale market. A very attractive boy cooks the cakes, who by the way is available."

Incredibly ugly and bestial women come down from the mountains carrying loads of charcoal on their backs. These are Berber women, unveiled, a blue tattoo stripe follows the cleft line from base of nose to upper lip, from lower lip to chin. Does the tattoo stripe continue along cleft line from cunt to asshole? I'm afraid we'll have to pigeonhole that under "Mysteries of the East." Our field man is a swish. . . . I notice many of these old charcoal beasts have their noses eaten away.

Two fags passing noseless woman: "My dear, these people lose their noses through sheer carelessness."

Interzone is crawling with pedophiles, citizens hung up on prepuberty kicks. I don't dig it. I say anyone can't wait till thirteen is no better than a degenerate.

Above notes under file head T.B.W.I.—To Be Weaved In . . . A routine starts here concerning a rich writer who employs an extensive staff to do menial work like "weaving." I have a group of men and women, "My Eager Little Beavers" as I call them. . . . So this writer is a sadistic tyrant, you dig? I come and supervise the work, maintaining the nauseous fiction they really are beavers, and they have to wear beaver suits and stand for a roll call . . . "Sally Beaver, Marvin Beaver," et cetera, et cetera.

"And watch you don't get caught when a tree falls," I say jovially, holding up a finger stub.

Sort of a horrible tour de force, like the books of Anthony Burgess. Nobody gives those people who write children's books credit for what they have to go through. I have discovered a certain writer of children's books is a great Kafkian figure. He chose to hide himself in children's stories as a joke.

For example, there was a story of Old Grumpy Stubbs, who said he needed subsidiary personalities—Subs, he calls them—to keep his psyche cleaned out and perform other menial chores around the "farm."

"So just sign here, my friend. You'll never regret this as long as you live."

But poor Albrecht the woodcutter did regret it as soon as he got back to his little proviso apartment—that is, an apartment that has already been leased to someone else, or on which the lease has expired, so you can only hope to stall a few days until they get the necessary papers for dispossessing you. Albrecht had lived in provisos all his life.

Well, even though he couldn't read Clause 9(v) of the contract—which can only be deciphered with an electron microscope and a virus filter—Albrecht knew somehow he had done a terrific thing to sell out to Old Stubbs, so called because he had cut off all but two of his fingers in an effort to amuse his constituents: "I get it back!" he would say, jovially rubbing his mutilated hands together. "I get it back!"

"I just don't know," Albrecht reflected. "Now Old Stubbs he talks real nice and he did cut off a thumb for me. . . . It isn't every Sub can say he got a thumb off the old man. Some of them didn't get nothing."

An Advertising Short for Television:

"So there they are, these two young kids, naked in a jungle clearing under a great, cheesy moon so big and close, like a big soft white ass, you dig me? Like you could reach right up and goose it, and all around the myriad sounds of the jungle night. They have found the Lost City in each other's arms.

"Well, do they get living et by mosquitoes?" (These lapses into faulty syntax are carefully cultivated by J.R., the Director. He is starting a J.R. legend, you dig?) "Do they wake up in the morning with their assholes swoll shut they can't shit? Not at all. They wake up in the magic of a jungle morning. A cool breeze gooses them gently, running light fingers over their lean, hard young bodies. Half in sleep, they begin to move in rhythmic contractions. . . .

"Well, the Hays Office steps in here, boys. They would have stepped in last night, but the Assistant Coordinate Censor fell out of the launch watching an Indian boy jack off in his dugout, and a *candiru* skedaddled up his prick and we had to roust out a witch man to extract the little varmint." (The *candiru* is a little eel-like critter about two inches long by one-quarter inch in diameter, that darts up your prick, ass, or a woman's cunt if he can't do any better, holding himself *in situ* by barbs. Just what he figures to gain by this maneuver is not known, and no martyrs have stepped forward to study the *candiru*'s life cycle on location.)

"So why aren't they attacked by the whining hordes? Does love protect them? Balls! They use the new DuPont 8-hour B-22 Insect Repellent, that's why. You too can shit or fuck in comfort from the jungles of Madagascar to the great Arctic marshes of Lapland, where the mosquitoes drink deep under the sword of Damocles like in a British pub: 'Hurry up please, it's time . . .' "

Antonio the Portuguese Mooch

The Portuguese mooch came and sat down with Lee. Lee glanced up and said: "Hello, Antonio. Sit down." He went on writing and ignored the demanding waves emanating from Antonio. Antonio compressed his lips and sighed. He clapped tiny hands which were the blue-purple color of poor circulation. He ordered a glass of water, turning his simian profile to ignore the waiter's look of cold contempt.

"Bill, I hate to bother you with the tragedies of my life. The life of a European filled with sickness and hunger." He coughed. "Americans are not able to understand these things. . . . You—stupid, vulgar, mechanized . . . How we *hate* you." He patted Lee's arm and smiled, showing his dirty, cheap false teeth. "Not you, of course. You are different from the other Americans. You have a heart at least."

"Yes. And liver and lungs and a stomach. What's on your greasy mind? As if I didn't know . . ."

Antonio did not notice. He was looking into space, his face twisted with monkey-like hate.

"Yah! To you Americans I am just a little performing monkey who will do dirty little tricks for a penny. *Less* than a penny . . . I remember when I am fourteen years old, two drunken American merchant marines have me to jack off at their café table in a crowded street in Lisbon. 'Guess I win the bet, Joe.' 'Yeah, I guess you do. I've seen everything now.' And he passed over a wad of escudos that would feed a Portuguese family for a year. 'How much is this in *money*, Joe?' He holds up a coin like this. . . ." Antonio made an ugly gesture, pinching thumb and forefinger together—Lee was used to Antonio, but sometimes the man gave him a shock with some indescribable twist of malevolent ugliness.

" 'Oh, about one fifth of a cent.'

" 'You think that's too much? I don't want to spoil him.'

" 'Oh hell. Might as well spread around a little goodwill.'

" 'Trouble is the little gook might go into convulsions of gratitude and die right here at the table. Haven't you got anything smaller?'

" 'Wait a minute. Yeah, here we are. Rock bottom. Throw it over there in that horse manure.' "

Antonio's imitation of American accents was perfect, like a

recording, but mixed. Brooklyn and Chicago, California, East Texas, Maine and the Deep South, the voice's absent owner appearing momentarily at the table, like a speeded-up superimposed movie.

The waiter set the glass of water down with a smack so that some of the water jumped out onto Antonio's sleeve. Antonio glared at the waiter, who flicked the table with a towel, then turned his back and walked away.

"Gratitude you want. We pick your coin out of dung with our teeth, and *then*, shit running down our chins, we should kiss your fine, long-wearing American boots, and say, 'Oh thank you, Johnny. Thank you for your generosity. . . . That you condescend to watch a European of noble family fuck his blood sister and that my performance could find favor in your sight. This I did not dare to hope for. . . . You are indeed kind. . . .' "

His voice rose to a piercing shriek. Lee looked up, vaguely annoyed.

"I, with seven-hundred-year-old blood in my veins! I, to kiss the feet of a son-of-a-bitch American peasant pig!"

He was spitting with rage, like an hysterical cat. Suddenly his plate flew out and he thrust his head forward, snapping for it. Lee glimpsed a horrible extension of Antonio's mouth, teeth on the end of a flesh tube, undulating across the table, silent, sinister and purposeful as a parasitic worm.

The plate slid across the table into Lee's lap. Lee flicked the plate back onto the table, snapping the cloth of his pants. Antonio picked it up and polished it on the tablecloth with one hand. With the other hand he kept his face covered. He replaced the teeth, kneading his face. Finally he turned on Lee a ghastly smile, his face yellow like dirty old wax, sweating with strain.

"But you are not like the other Americans. You are a . . . good guy."

"Did you ever think of working, young man?" Lee asked.

"In Tangier is no work."

"Well, I know the owner of the Café de la Paix. I might could get you on as a part-time lavatory attendant. After all, it's honest, respectable work, and there's a future in it. He's thinking of putting in a shoeshine parlor, and you might work right into a bootblack job. That is, if you apply yourself, keep your eye on the ball. . . . When an American finishes shitting, don't just stand there, wipe his ass. And wipe it better than it was ever wiped before."

Antonio glared at Lee. Lee smiled. His face ghastly with strain, hate streaming out of his eyes like a malevolent shortwave broadcast, Antonio smiled back.

"You are joking, Bill."

"Sure. We're great kidders, us Americans."

"Americans! They come to Europe and buy us like cattle! 'You're in the wrong hole, Clem. That's a he-gook you got there.' 'So what, Luke? 'Tain't as if it was being queer. After all, they's only gooks.'

"You cannot understand what it means, Bill. You do not come from an old family. To have seen my great-aunt Mitzi, the Dowager Countess of Borganzola, the proudest family in Europe, an old lady of eighty years, dancing the can-can for drunken American soldiers. 'Shake the lead out, grandma. I got money on your ass.' And I stand there helpless. I hate them so almost I cannot pass around the hat."

"Okay," Lee said. "I'll take over the script now. Your old mother is gaping like a fish, locked out of her iron lung for nonpayment of rent. The finance company is repossessing your wife's artificial kidney. . . . It's going to be tough, sitting there watching her swell up and turn black, drowning in her own piss, your darling wife, the mother of your dead son, last of the noble line of Borganzola, and the croaker said just one more day with the kidney and she is functioning again. A sad, sweet, resigned smile . . . 'Ah well

. . . My life has been one long tragedy. But to think that only fifty pesetas would save her! It is too cruel!'

"You express the dilemma of the European, Antonio. You hate us so much *almost* you cannot pass around the hat."

Displaced Fuzz

A drastic simplification of U.S. law has thrown thousands of cops and narcotics agents out of work: The DFs—Displaced Fuzz—overran the Placement Center, snarling and whimpering like toothless predators: "I don't ask much out of life. Just let me give *some* citizen a bad time."

A few of them were absorbed by Friendly Finance:

DF 1: "Now, lady, we wouldn't want to repossess the artificial kidney, what with your kid in such a condition like that, not being able to piss."

DF 2: "Anna innarest."

DF 1: "Anna carrying charges."

DF 2: "Anna upkeep."

DF 1: "Anna wear and tear onna appliance."

DF 2: "Depreciation, whyncha?"

DF 1: "Check, *and* the depreciation."

DF 2: "It's like you're delinquent already. . . . Mmmm. *Quite a gadget.*"

DF 1: "Quite a *gadget*."

DF 2: "Not the sort of thing you could make out of an old washing machine in your basement."

DF 1: "If you had an old washing machine."

DF 2: "Anna basement."

Lady: "But what am I to do? I been replaced by the automation."

DF 2: "I'm not Mr. Anthony, lady. . . ."

DF 1: "You might peddle the kid's ass if he'll stand still for it, haw haw haw. . . . Lady, we'd like to help you. . . . You see—"

DF 2: "—We got a job to do is all. You should be able to save sumpin'."

DF 1: "Maybe he pisses it all down the drain. Haw haw haw."

A DF can still get his kicks with Friendly Finance. But what about the other DFs?

One of them obtained a sinecure as lavatory attendant in a Greyhound terminal and maintained his self-respect by denouncing occasional improprieties and attempts to tamper with or circumvent the pay toilets. To this end he concealed himself in the towel receptacle, peeking out through a hinged slot.

Another worked in a Turkish bath and equipped himself with infrared binoculars: "All right, you there in the north corner. I see you." He couldn't actually denounce the clients or throw them out, but he did create such an unnerving ambiance—prowling about the halls, poking into the steam room, switching on floodlights, sticking his head into the cubicles through hinged panels in the walls and floors—that many a queen was carried out in a strait-jacket. So he lived out a full life and died at an advanced age of prostate cancer.

Another was not so fortunate. For a while he worked as a concierge, but he harried the tenants beyond endurance, so they finally banded together and were preparing to burn him alive in the furnace—which he habitually either over- or understoked—when the police intervened. He was removed from office for his own protection. He then secured a position as a subway guard, but was summarily dismissed for using a sharpened pole to push people into the cars during the rush hour. He subsequently worked as a bus driver, but his habit of constantly looking around to see what the passengers were doing precipitated a wreck, from which he emerged shattered in mind and body. He became a psychopathic informer, writing interminable letters to the FBI which J. Edgar used as toilet paper, being of a thrifty temperament. He sank ever lower and ended up Latah for cops, and would spend his days in front of any precinct that would tolerate his presence, having been barred from the area in and about Police Headquarters as a notorious bringdown.

Spare Ass Annie

When I became captain of the town, I decided to extend asylum to certain citizens who were persona non grata elsewhere in the area because of their disgusting and disquieting deformities.

One was known as Spare Ass Annie. She had an auxiliary asshole in the middle of her forehead, like a baneful bronze eye. Another was a scorpion from the neck down. He had retained the human attribute of voice and was given to revolting paroxysms of self-pity and self-disgust during which he would threaten to kill himself by a sting in the back of the neck. He never threatened anyone else, though his sting would have caused instant death.

Another, and by far the most detrimental, was like a giant centipede, but terminated in human legs and lower abdomen. Sometimes he walked half-erect, his centipede body swaying ahead of him. At other times he crawled, dragging his human portion as an awkward burden. At first sight he looked like a giant, crippled centipede. He was known as the Centipeter, because he was continually making sexual advances to anyone he could corner, and anyone who passed out was subject to wake up with Centipete in his bed. One degenerate hermaphrodite known as Fish Cunt Sara claimed he was the best lay in town: "Besides, he's a perfect gentleman in every sense of the word. He's kind and good, which means nothing to the likes of you. . . ."

These creatures had developed in a region where the priests

carried out strange rites. They built boxes from the moist, fresh bones of healthy youths, captives from neighboring tribes. The boys were killed by looping a vine noose around their necks and pushing them off the branch of a giant cypress tree. The branch had been cut off and carved in the form of an enormous phallus, being some fifteen feet long and three feet in circumference. The vine (always a *yagé* plant) was attached to the end of the branch, and the youth was led out and pushed off so that he fell about eight feet, breaking his neck. Then the priests pounced on him, while he was still twitching in orgasmic convulsions, and cut through the flesh with copper knives, tearing out the bones. From these bones they made boxes with great skill and speed, lining the boxes with copper. Runners were dispatched to carry the boxes to a certain high peak where peculiar lights were given off by the rocks. Pregnant women were placed in the boxes and left on the peak for a period of three hours. Often the women died, but those who survived usually produced monsters. The priests considered these monstrosities a way of humiliating the human race before the gods, in the hope of diverting their anger.

These horrible freaks were highly prized, and they lived in the temple. The women who gave birth to the most monsters received gold stars, which they were authorized to wear on ceremonial occasions.

Once a month they held a great festival at which everyone gathered in a round stone temple, open at the top, and prostrated themselves on the floor, assuming the most disgusting and degraded positions possible, so that the gods would see they were not attempting to elevate themselves above their station.

The habit of living in filth and humiliation finally occasioned a plague, a form of acute leprosy, that depopulated the area. The surviving freaks (who seemed immune to the plague) I decided to receive as an object lesson in how far human kicks can go.

The Dream Cops

There was a sudden thunder of knocks on the door. The Agent pulled on his trousers and turned the key in the lock. Three men pushed into the room. Two were in plain clothes, one in uniform. The man in uniform immediately pulled a pair of handcuffs out of his pocket and twisted them around the Agent's wrists. The handcuffs were made of a tough pliable wood. His uniform was torn and spotted, the tunic twisted and buttoned in the wrong holes.

One of the plainclothesmen looked like a vaudeville-house detective, with derby and cigar. The cigar was ten inches long. The other plainclothesman was tall and thin and carried an instrument that looked like a slide rule.

"The cigar's too long," said the Agent. "A dream cigar. You can't touch me."

The house detective nodded to the uniformed cop. The cop showed dirty steel teeth in a snarl. He hit the Agent across the mouth. The Agent could taste the blood.

"You have some peculiar dreams," said the detective. "Besides, we can dream too. . . . Sleeping with a nigger."

The Agent was about to deny this, but when he turned to look there was a young Negro in his bed. Huge lice crawled in and out of the Negro's greasy, frizzled hair.

"All right," said the detective. "Let's see your arm."

The Agent rolled up the sleeve of his sweatshirt. Sparks exploded behind his eyes. Blood ran down his chin. He got up, looking at the house detective.

"Wise guy, eh?" the house detective snarled, his eyes phosphorescent, his mouth slavering. "You're the wisest prick I ever walked in on. Let's see your *arm*. Your *short* arm."

He reached out a hairy hand as thick as it was wide, and grabbed the Agent's belt. With the other hand he ripped open the Agent's fly. The buttons rolled across the floor. He held the Agent's penis judicially between thumb and forefinger. He turned to the other plainclothesman—glen-plaid suit, skin tight and smooth and red over his face, bad teeth. Smoking a cigar shaped like a cigarette. He had been taking down the number on the Agent's kerosene stove.

"Sixty percent of them are Jews," said the house detective.

"I'm not Jewish," said the Agent.

"Sure, I know. You fucked one of those characters eats glass and razor blades and circumscribed yourself. Not Jewish!"

The other detective looked up from the kerosene stove and laughed sycophantically. A gold filling fell out on the floor.

At a signal from the house detective, the uniformed cop took the handcuffs off.

"Watch your step," said the house detective. The three men went out, closing the door.

Next morning the Agent's mouth was still sore. Lighting the kerosene stove, he found a gold filling.

THE CONSPIRACY

Yes, they know we'll wait. How many hours, days, years, street corners, cafeterias, furnished rooms, park benches, sitting, standing, walking? . . . All those who wait know that time and space are one. How long-far to the end of the block and back? How many games of solitaire make an hour? . . . Then time will suddenly jump, slip ahead. This happens usually in the late afternoon, after four o'clock. From one to four you hit on the slowest time.

I was reexamining candidates, proceeding by elimination, to isolate the name. Yes, I thought, that is correct procedure. At the same time, I knew the name would probably be a dark horse, someone I hadn't thought of, like the man who says, "Why didn't you come to me? I'd have lent you the money," and you know he would have lent it. It was someone like that I was looking for, while the logical elimination of prospects went on:

Gardiner? I wonder how he would manage to turn me in without picking up a phone and calling the law? By getting arrested himself? By telling someone who was sure to talk?

Marvin? At least he would say: "Bill, I can't do it. I won't take the risk. You'll have to get out."

Anyone who would do it for money was out. There would be more money on the other side. Two cops. That can scare up $5,000 overnight. (Why is killing a cop such a heinous crime in America? It isn't so in Mexico or South America. Because Americans accept cops at their own valuation, as they accept anyone who has the means of force.)

"Not a man of my acquaintance, that I'm sure of. . . ."

("Is this your final report?")

Not a man . . . not a man. . . . Well, how about a woman? . . . A woman? Well . . . Mary! That was the name, the answer.

I told the driver to stop. We were passing 72nd Street. I got out, paid the cab back to Washington Square, and waved good-bye to Nick, still in the cab.

I took the subway up to 116th Street and walked across the Columbia campus to Mary's flat. Why didn't I think of her first? A university campus—the perfect hideout. And I could count on Mary, count on her 100 percent. The building was a four-story brownstone. The windows shone clean and black in the morning sunlight. I walked up three flights and knocked on the door. Mary opened it and stood there looking at me.

"Come in," she said, her face lighting up. "Want a cup of coffee?" I sat down with her at the kitchen table and drank coffee and ate a piece of coffee cake.

"Mary, I want to hide out here for a while. I don't know how long exactly. You can say someone rented the extra room to write his thesis. He doesn't want to go out of the room or see anyone till it's finished. You have to buy his food and bring it to him. He's paying you one hundred dollars to stay there three weeks, or however long it takes. I just killed two detectives."

Mary lit a cigarette. "Holdup?"

"No. It's much more complicated than that. Let's move to the living room, in case somebody comes. I'll tell you about it. . . .

"Light junk sickness, when I wake up needing a shot, always gives me a sharp feeling of nostalgia, like train whistles, piano music down a city street, burning leaves. . . . I mentioned this to you, didn't I?"

Mary nodded. "Several times."

"An experience we think of as fleeting, incalculable, coming and going in response to unknown factors. But the feeling appears without fail, in response to a definite metabolic setup. It's possible to find out exactly what that setup is and reproduce it at will, given sufficient knowledge of the factors involved. Conversely it is possible to eliminate nostalgia, to occlude the whole dreaming, symbolizing faculty."

"And you mean it's been done?"

"Exactly. Scientists have perfected the anti-dream drug, which is, logically, a synthetic variation on the junk theme. . . . And the drug is habit forming to a point where one injection can cause lifelong addiction. If the addict doesn't get his shot every eight hours he dies in convulsions of oversensitivity."

"Like nerve gas."

"Similar. In short, once you are hooked on the anti-dream drug, you can't get back. Withdrawal symptoms are fatal. Users are dependent for their lives on the supply, and at the same time, the source of resistance, contact with the myth that gives each man the ability to live alone and unites him with all other life, is cut off. He becomes an automaton, an interchangeable quantity in the political and economic equation."

"Is there an antidote?"

"Yes. More than that, there is a drug that increases the symbolizing faculty. It's a synthetic variation of telepathine or yageine, the active principle of *Bannisteria caapi*."

"And where do you come in?" Mary asked.

"Five years ago I made a study of *Bannisteria caapi*—the Indians called it Yagé, Ayauhuasca, Pilde—in South America, and found out something about the possible synthetic variations. The symbolizing or artistic faculty that some people are born with—though almost everyone has it to some degree as a child—can be increased a hundred times. We can all be artists infinitely greater than Shakespeare or Beethoven or Michelangelo. Because this is possible, the opposite is also possible. We can be deprived of symbol-making power, a whole dimension excised, reduced to completely rational nonsymbolizing creatures. Perhaps . . ."

"Yes?"

"I was wondering whether . . . Well, let it go. We have enough to think about."

That afternoon Mary went out and bought the papers. There was no mention of Hauser and O'Brien.

"When they can keep that quiet they must have a fix in near the top. With the ordinary apparatus of law looking for me, I might have one chance in a hundred; this way . . ."

I told Mary to go to a pay phone in Times Square, call police headquarters and ask for Hauser. Then go across the street and see what happens. She was back in half an hour.

"Well?"

She nodded. "They stalled me, said to hang on a minute, he was on the way. So I cut across the street. Not more than three minutes later a car was there. Not a police car. They blocked both entrances to the drugstore—I called from the drugstore—two went in and checked the phone booths. I could see them questioning the clerk, and he was saying in pantomime: 'How should I know? A thousand people in and out of here every day.' "

"And now you're convinced I'm not having a pipe dream? I wish I *could* have one. Haven't seen any gum in a dog's age. . . ."

"So what do we do now?"

"I don't know. I'd better start at the beginning and bring you up to date."

What was the beginning? Since early youth I had been searching for some secret, some key by which I could gain access to basic knowledge and answer some of the fundamental questions. Just what I was looking for, what I meant by basic knowledge or fundamental questions, I found it difficult to define. I would follow a trail of clues. For example, the pleasure of drugs to the addict is relief from the state of drug need. Perhaps all pleasure is relief and could be expressed by a basic formula. Pleasure must be proportional to the discomfort or tension from which it is the relief. This holds for the pleasure of junk. You never know what pleasure is until you are really junk-sick.

Drug addiction is perhaps a basic formula for pleasure and for life itself. That is why the habit, once contracted, is so difficult to break, and why it leaves, when broken, such a vacuum behind. The addict has glimpsed the formula, the bare bones of life, and this knowledge has destroyed for him the ordinary sources of satisfaction that make life endurable. To go a step further, to find out exactly what tension is, and what relief, to discover the means of manipulating these factors . . . The final key always eluded me, and I decided that my search was as sterile and misdirected as the alchemists' search for the philosopher's stone. I decided it was an error to think in terms of some secret or key or formula: the secret is that there is no secret.

But I was wrong. There *is* a secret, now in the hands of ignorant and evil men, a secret beside which the atomic bomb is a noisy toy. And like it or not, I was involved. I had already ante'd my life. I had no choice but to sit the hand out.

IRON WRACK DREAM

This is one of the worst habits I ever kicked. I sit for an hour in a chair, unable to get up and fix myself a cup of tea.

Early this morning, half awake, shivering in a light junk-sick fever, I had a vivid dream-fantasy. The hypersensitivity of junk sickness is reflected in dreams during withdrawal—that is, if you can sleep.

In the dream, I go to an elaborate house on a high cliff over the sea. An iron door opens in a limestone cliff, and you get to the house in a swift, silent elevator.

I have come to see a sexless character who wears men's clothes but may be man or woman. Nobody knows for sure. A gangster of the future, with official recognition and arbitrary powers.

He walks toward me as if about to shake hands. He does not offer his hand. "Hello," he says. "Hello . . . there."

The room is surrounded on three sides by a transparent plastic shell.

"You will want to see the view," he says. A plastic panel slides back. I step out onto a limestone terrace cut from the solid rock of the cliff. No rail or wall. A heavy mist, but from time to time I can see the waves breaking on the rocks a thousand feet below. See the waves, but I don't hear them, like a silent film. Two bodyguards are standing a few feet behind me.

"It gives the sensation of flying," I say.

"Sometimes."

"Well, feller say only angels have wings," I say recklessly. I turn around. I say, "Excuse me." The bodyguards don't move. They are standing with their backs to him. He is arranging flowers in an obscene alabaster bowl. The guards cannot see him and he says nothing, makes no sound, but a signal has been given. The guards step aside to let me pass, back into the room.

I walk up to the table where he is arranging flowers. "I want to know where Jim is," I say.

"Mmm. Yes. I suppose you do."

"Will you tell me?"

"Maybe Jim doesn't want to see you."

"If he doesn't, I want to hear it from him."

"I never give anything for nothing. I want your room in the Chimu. I want you out of there by nine tomorrow morning."

"All right."

"Go to 60 at Fourth Street, coordinate 20, level 16, YH room 72."

The City is a vast network of levels, like the Racks, connected by gangways and cars that run on wires and single tracks. You put a coin in a vacant car and it will take you anywhere on its track or wire. Everyone carries an instrument called a coordinator, to orient himself.

The City is in the U.S. The forces of evil and repression have run their course here. They are suffocating in their armor or exploding from inner pressure. New forms of life are germinating in the vast, rusty metal racks of the ruined City.

It takes me twelve hours to find the address. A padded hammer hangs from a copper chain on the door. I knock.

A man comes to the door: bald, looks like an old actor on the skids. Effeminate, but not queer. A dumpy, middle-aged woman is sitting in a purple velvet brocaded chair left over from 1910. She looks good-natured. I say I want to see Jim.

"And *who* might you be?" the man asks.

"I'm Bill."

He laughs. "He's Bill, Gertie." He turns to me. "Someone was just here asking for Bill."

"How long ago?"

"Just five minutes," the woman says.

"Can I stay five minutes?" I ask. "I mean, if someone was here five minutes ago asking for *Bill,* and now I am here asking for *Jim* . . . well . . ."

"You don't have to *slug* me with it," the man says. "But I never heard of Bill or Jim."

"Oh, let him stay," the woman says.

Five minutes later there is a knock. The man opens the door.

"Hello," he says. "You wouldn't be Jim, by any chance?"

"Yes, I'm Jim. I'm looking for Polly."

"Polly doesn't live here anymore." The man sings it.

Jim sees me. "Hello, Bill," he says. He smiles and cancels all the reproaches I had stored up.

"Let's go, Jim," I say, standing up. I turn to the man and woman. "Thanks for your trouble."

"Anytime, old thing," the man says. He is about to say something more.

"That's okay, boys," the woman cuts in.

We walk out together. "I need a drink," Jim says. We find a bar and sit down in a booth. There is no one else in the place. Jim is beautiful but has the kind of face that shows every day that much older. There are circles under his eyes, like bruises. He drinks five double Scotches. He is sweet and gentle when drunk. I help him out of the bar. We go to my room and sleep there.

Next morning I throw the few things I have—mostly photos and manuscripts—into a plastic bag, and we leave.

Jim has a place on a roof. You unlock a metal door and climb four flights of rusty, precarious stairs. One room with a mattress, a table and a chair. Metal walls. A toilet in one corner, a gas stove in another. A tap dripping into a sink.

Jim is trembling convulsively. "I'm scared, Bill," he says over and over.

I hold him, and stroke his head, and undress him.

We sleep together until twelve that night. We wake up and dress and Jim makes coffee. We take turns drinking from a tin can.

We start out looking for Polly. Jim gives me an extra key to his place, before we leave the room.

The City is honeycombed with nightclubs and bars. Many of them change locations every night. The nightclubs are underground, hanging from cables, and built on perilous balconies a thousand feet over the rubbish and rusty metal of the City.

We make the rounds, and we find Polly in Cliff's place. The room shifts from time to time, with a creak of metal. It is built in a rusty tower that sways in the wind. "This place is too good to last, kids," Cliff says, laughing.

Polly is a dark Jewish girl. She looks like that picture of Allen Ginsberg on the beach when he was three years old. Jim is talking to some people at the bar. I put the key in her hand and press it there. She kisses me lightly on the lips and then on the ear, murmuring, "Billy Boy . . ."

I find a car and ride down to the waterfront. I see a light. A man is standing in a doorway.

"You open?" I ask.

"Why not?"

I go in. The place is empty. I sit at a table. He brings me a soft drink without asking what I want, and sits down at the table opposite me. A gentle, thuggish face, broken nose, battered but calm and kind.

"Where you live at?" he asks me.

"No place now."

"Want to shack up here?"

"Why not?" I finish my drink and he leads the way to a round metal door that opens soundlessly on oiled bearings. He motions for me to go in. His hand rests on my shoulder, and slides down my ass with a gentle forward pat.

GINSBERG NOTES

Lee woke again. The room was light now. He could hear the clock ticking, but he did not want to look at it, to locate himself definitely in time, to be completely awake. He arranged the covers to shade his eyes, pushing them away from his mouth so he could breathe comfortably. A shiver ran through his body. He closed his eyes, remembering his dream, clinging to sleep.

He had been dreaming about marshmallows. He had four or five marshmallows, and he was preparing to toast them in little wooden boxes which had wicks running around the edges like a kerosene stove. The dream had a tone of furtive, but overpowering, sexuality.

What's sexy about marshmallows? he thought, irritably. He felt aware of his sexual organs, but not in the normal manner of sexual excitement. It was as if he could feel inside the whole genitourinary apparatus, the intolerable, febrile sexuality of junk sickness.

Marshmallows, boxes . . . cunts, of course. Mary, the English governess . . . dreams of something sticky in his mouth, like chewing gum. The memory he never could reoccupy, even under deep narcoanalysis. Whenever he got close to it, excitation tore through him, suppressed below the level of emotional coloring, a neutral energy like electricity. The memory itself never actually seen or reexperienced, only delineated by refusals, disgusts, negation. He knew, of course, what it must be, but the knowledge was of the brain only.

He shivered again, feeling the discordant twang of unfamiliar visceral sensations, the light fever of sickness. The Spanish word *escalofríos* came to him, then the English "chills and fever," hot and cold. Every moment he felt more intolerably conscious. He looked at the clock: eight-thirty. It was always slow—it was nearer to nine.

Soon the drugstores will open. If only the methadone comes through today. If only I could get my money so I can get to England and take the cure.

If only his body had never known junk. How could he ever unknow it? He decided he would settle for a cure and then a place to live where it is never cold.

No use trying to sleep any longer. He pushed the covers aside and sat up. Immediately he began to shiver. He crossed the room and lit a small kerosene stove, with trembling hands. He reached into an open drawer and took out a small syringe filled with colorless liquid.

He held the syringe poised, and looked down at his blue hands, coldly, impersonally. *No use trying to hit there*, he decided. He felt along the side of his bare foot. *There's one I might be able to hit*. He pushed the needle in his foot at the ankle, feeling, probing for a vein. Pain swept through his sensitized flesh. A thin column of blood climbed sluggishly into the syringe. He pressed the plunger. The liquid went in very slowly. Every now and then his foot twitched involuntarily away from the needle, which was embedded almost to the point where it joined the syringe.

The last of the liquid drained in. He pulled out the needle and stopped the blood with a piece of cotton. He sat listening down into his viscera, waiting for the effect.

Lee had discovered that he got his best ideas while lying in bed with a young boy after the fact. At first he thought this was coincidence. *God damn it, every time I get ideas for writing, I am occupied with a boy. Or maybe it's the other way around . . . hmm. Weel, I'm in the right place.*

He embarked on a three-thousand-page sexology, as he called it. One after the other his boys were drained of their orgones and cast aside, dragging themselves about like terminal hookworm-malaria-malnutrition cases.

"I don't know why, but I just feel sorta tired after I make it with that writing feller."

"You can say that again, Pepe. And in all my experience man and boy as a grade-A five-star hustler—A.J. gives me five stars in his Sex and Drug Guide—I never yet see a citizen type and get fucked at the same time. You shoulda seen me before I met Lee. I was a good-looking kid, had all my hair and teeth. I'm only twenty-four—well, twenty-nine. Shucks, we're in the same line. . . . I can afford to let my hair down a bit, that is, if I had any. . . ."

I figure it will require the orgones of ten thousand boys to finish my sexology. I assume the frightful responsibility of the creative artist.

A group of rich queens formed a corporation and offered a reward of one million dollars to any assassin who would dispose of "this shameless liquefactionist, who is debauching and decanting our boys—oh, uh, I mean the youth of the world."

There are two middle-aged, ugly, fattish men in a club like the University Club or the Harvard Club. The two are on cordial but by no means familiar terms.

Scene is the club sitting-room. The other members are annoyed, you understand, by anyone even talking there, as they want to sit and think about their money and doze and digest. We will call them Jack and Robert.

Jack: "Let's rekindle the embers!"

Robert: "Huh? The embers of precisely what?"

Jack: "Don't tell me you've forgotten our nights on the sandbanks of the Putumayo with the piranha fish jumping out there in the soft tropic darkness. All around us the brooding jungle of the Amazon, like a great carnivorous plant. It was Auca country, but we were drunk with youth and love. We laughed at danger and perhaps the Auca laughed with us and lowered their poison arrows and stole away into the jungle. And the moon so clear you could read by it—why, I can see you now, lying there with your beautiful mouth a little open, clad only in youth and innocence."

Robert: "I'm damned if you can! For one thing, I've never been within a thousand miles of the Amazon!"

Jack: "And remember that waterfall back in the virgin jungle of the upper Shipibo? We'd been walking all day since sun-up, hacking our way through with machetes. And you said it was my fault we'd missed the way, and sulked for ten hours. You always looked beautiful when you were sulky. And then we broke through the jungle to a crystal-clear river and a waterfall so high the top was lost in mist, and we stripped off our clothes and played under the waterfall until the sun went down and the mosquitoes came out with the moon."

Robert: "What are you talking about?"

Jack: "Let's go up to my room and play touchies!"

Robert: "Play what!"

Jack: "Touchies! *Our* little game!"

Robert: "Listen. I've had just about enough of your silly games, and since you lead me to say so, Throckmorton, I strongly advise you to see an able psychiatrist without delay."

Jack: "Ah well, perhaps it wasn't in the Amazon . . . come to think of it. We were just kids, fourteen, fifteen. It was in a deserted house down by the railroad tracks. We made a great thing of breaking into the house, and you looked at me solemnly and said: 'Do you realize we're burglars?' And there was an old mattress on the floor in a dark room with the shutters nailed down, and we dragged the mattress into the middle of the room and wrestled on it, and you won, as you always did, and I lay there looking up at you and a train whistled in the distance and we took off our clothes in the musty darkness. It was like the pure blue flame of a welder's torch: sudden, hot, intense in both of us. . . . Later we walked home at twilight along the tracks, a beautiful clear Indian summer day, and we were so happy we didn't say anything all the way home, with our arms around each other's necks, so young it never occurred to either of us anyone would think anything about it. And when we got back to the main road it was dark, with a full moon rising red over the smokestacks of the city and the smell of burning leaves in the air. . . ."

Robert: "You obviously have me confused with someone else. Now if you will excuse me."

Jack: "Wait a minute! It all comes back now. . . . I had a little studio apartment on Jane Street in the Village. It was my first time really away from home and on my own. I was young, I had a secondhand Remington, I was going to write the Great American

Novel. So what difference did it make if the bed was lumpy, and the windowpane vibrated in a raw winter wind, and the radiator gave off more noise than heat, and a black dust seeped into the room and covered my manuscripts, my clothes, my pillow, and got in my hair and ears so I always looked a little dirty? I was happy, and deadly serious about my writing, and I believed in my talent.

"But I was desperately lonely. I had read Oscar Wilde and Gide and Proust and Havelock Ellis. I knew that I was destined to love my own sex as long as I lived. I accepted this. After all, so many great writers had been like that. I used to go out after writing all day, every night to a different bar, always hoping to meet someone who would understand what I was trying to say on paper, who would share my lumpy bed, and we would wake up in the cold, gray dawn, warm with each other's bodies.

"Then one night I happened into a strange, equivocal place on Twelfth Street at Second Avenue. It was called The Clock Bar. The Clock had no regular crowd. It was not bohemian or tough or Bowery. It was a place where anyone could happen in. The place was empty—except for you. . . ."

Take it up from the next page. You can carry this second-rate-novel kick too far. I just got writing and couldn't stop.

When a depressed psychotic begins to recover, that is, when recovery becomes possible, the illness makes a final all-out attack, and this is the point of maximum suicide danger. You might say the human race is now at this point, in a position for the first time, by virtue of knowledge which may destroy us, to step free of self-imposed restrictions and see all life as a fact. When you see the world direct, everything is a delight, and boredom or unhappiness is impossible.

The forces of negation and death are now making their all-out suicidal effort. The citizens of the world are helpless in a paranoid panic. First one thing and then another is seen as the enemy, while the real enemy hesitates—perhaps because it looks too easy, like an ambush. Among the Arabs and the East in general, the West (especially America), or domination by foreigners, is seen as the enemy. In the West: communism, queers, drug addicts.

Queers have been worked over by female Senders. They are a reminder of what the Senders can and will do unless they are stopped. Also many of them have sold out their bodies to Death, Inc. Their souls wouldn't buy a paper of milk sugar shit. But the enemy needs bodies to get around.

Also there is no doubt some drugs condition one to receive, that is, soften one up for the Senders. Junk is not such a drug, but it is a prototype of invasion. That is, junk replaces the user cell by cell until he *is* junk, so the Sender will invade and replace until separate life is destroyed. Nothing but fact can save us, and Einstein is the first prophet of fact. Anyone is free, of course, to deliberately choose insanity and say that the universe is square or heart-shaped, but it is, as a matter of fact, curved.

Similar facts: morality (at this point an unqualified evil), ethics, philosophy, religion, can no longer maintain an existence separate from facts of physiology, bodily chemistry, LSD, electronics, physics. Psychology no longer exists, since a science of mind has no meaning. Sociology and all the so-called social sciences are suspect to be purveyors of pretentious gibberish.

The next set of facts of similar import will most likely come from present research on schizophrenia, the electronics of hallucination and the metabolism of insanity, cancer, the behavior and nature of viruses—and possibly drug addiction as a microcosm of life, pleasure and human purpose. It is also from such research that the greatest danger to the human race will come—probably has already come—a danger greater than the atom bomb, because more likely to be misunderstood.

I am taking another junk cure—is this my tenth or eleventh cure? I forget—in the Hassan Hospital of Interzone. They are curing me slow, and why not? Stateside croakers are mostly puritan sadists, who feel a junky *should* suffer taking the cure. Here they look at it differently.

I could never have been a doctor. I did right to quit. My heart is too soft and too hard, too quickly moved to love, anger, or indifference. I would care too much for some patients and nothing for others: Like I mess a case up and kill some jerk, so I say: "It's all in the day's work. Get this stiff outa here. I'm waiting on another patient."

People talk about "the hospital smell." You never had it till you sniff a Spanish hospital. All the old standbys: ether, carbolic, alcohol, the antiseptic, ozone smell of bandages *plus* piss and shit and dirty babies, cunts with the rag on, never-washed pricks, sweat and garlic, saffron and olive oil, afterbirths, gangrene, *keif* and death.

I used to be in room 10 and they moved me upstairs. Just passed my old room, where they had a maternity case, looks like. Terrible mess and bedpans full of blood and Kotex and nameless female substances enough to pollute a continent. Just thought, suppose somebody comes to visit me in my old room, they will think I give birth to a monster, and the State Department is trying to hush it up.

Dave Dunlop just came in, and I was telling him about the eels. It was a Dane found out about them. Gave his whole life to the eels—it would be a Dane, somehow. When the adult eels reach the Sargasso Sea, which is actually a place in the Atlantic, they go down into it and disappear. It is assumed they mate and die down there—nobody has seen them doing either—but sure as shit an eel doesn't come all that distance and lose his ass in the service for no purpose.

Often pain and death leave me untouched. I have seen hundreds of bullfights. I feel nothing for the bull. The old man who died a few days ago just annoyed me with his groans. He had the stupid, blunted look of a sick cow. Some people would call me callous, but I am not so. It is simply that I divide people into those who matter and those who do not, and I have no concern with quantitative criteria. If I do feel someone else's pain, I feel it with my whole being. It shatters me. I just heard a child screaming downstairs, and tears came to my eyes. I can't stand the pain of children. No, I could never have been a doctor. I would be crying over some child while people I didn't like died in the hall.

More trouble with the Evil Night Nurse. I caught her *in flagrante* cutting my shot in half with water. I don't say nothing. Later she doesn't even bother to cut it. Just brings me a shot of two ampules, instead of four like she's supposed.

I say: "That's two centimeters."

She say: "No, it's four. The syringe is bigger."

I say: "Look, *señorita*" (she's no more *señorita* than I am. Brazen old junky cunt)—"I got eyes. I want four centimeters."

"I can't give you any more."

"All right, *señorita*. I'll be having a little talk with the croaker *mañana*."

See what I mean? I give her a chance to come up right. If she told me straight, "I got a habit. You know how it is," I would say, "All right. All right. Just fuck up somebody else's shot."

But she gives me a snow job. Well, I'm going to fix her wagon good.

Yesterday I meant to add a few sentences to this. Possessed by a wild routine and wrote two pages. I laughed till my stomach hurt.

These routines will reduce me to a cinder, like the Technician. And how can I ever write a "novel"? I can't and won't. The "novel" is a dead form, rigid and arbitrary. I can't use it.

The chapters form a mosaic, with the dream impact of juxtaposition, like objects abandoned in a hotel drawer, a form of still life. Just looking over Chapter II. I don't know. The mosaic method is more suitable to painting than writing. I mean, you can *see* a painting as a whole.

What I want to do in Chapter II is to indicate Lee's literal point of view. The following concepts are central:

1. He writes with horror and foreboding because his writing is meant to be acted out somewhere, somehow, sometime, and so can put him in actual danger.

2. Repetition of Lee's desire and intention to kick habit. Junk keeps him in state of suspension. He must kick to realize his routines. His cautious, junk-bound flesh is reluctant to leave the safety of junk. I notice the songs that sing themselves in my head indicate my hesitancy to leave the safe, warm place of junk. One for example: I heard the tune a long time before I remembered the words. It's about an old spade who has sold his "cabin and patch of ground" to go north for better pay:

"But Dinah she don't want to go
She says we're getting old
She's 'fraid that she will freeze to death
The country am so cold
That story 'bout the work and pay
She don't believe it's true
She begs me not to do the thing
That I am bound to do."

Dinah is junk, of course—that is, my cellular representative of junk.

3. His love for anyone is always a pretext, a means to achieve something, to go somewhere. . . . Perhaps the search for an ideal audience?

4. The Routine (Birth of the Monster, Hassan the Afterbirth King, the Baboon Stick, etc.) as Lee's special form. What distinguishes the routine from writing, painting, music? It is *not completely symbolic* but subject to slide over into action at any time. (Cutting off finger joint, wrecking the car, etc. In a sense, the whole Nazi movement was a great, humorless, evil *routine* on Hitler's part.) Routines are uncontrollable, unpredictable, charged with potential danger for Lee himself, and anyone close to him is liable to be caught in the line of fire. I mean the so-called innocent bystanders. Actually there are no "innocent bystanders." In the immortal words of Huncke, "We are all guilty of everything."

Of all forms, the routine is closest to bullfighting. The routine artist is always trying to outdo himself, to go a little further, to commit some incredible but appropriate excess. A routine, like a bullfight, needs an audience. In fact the audience is an integral part of the routine. But unlike a bullfight, the routine can endanger the audience.

This morning the orderly took my table away to surgery. I opened my knife and held it out to him: "Need this too?" I'm the life of the hospital.

A wet dream of a thirteen-year-old redheaded kid waiting for treatment, sitting on the long white waiting bench . . . I see myself a doctor, bandaging his thigh with "sweet, reluctant, amorous delay."

"Mrs. Brounswig is in shock, Doctor. I can't find her pulse."

"Maybe she's got it up her snatch in a finger stall."

"Adrenalin, doctor?"

"The night porter shot it all up for kicks."

Tangier extends in several dimensions. You keep finding places you never saw before. There is no line between "real world" and "world of myth and symbol." Objects, sensations, hit with the impact of hallucination. Of course I see now with the child's eyes, the Lazarus eyes of return from the gray Limbo of junk. But what I see is there. Others see it too.

I am selecting, editing and transcribing letters and notes from the past year, some typed, some indecipherable longhand, for Chapter II of my novel on Interzone, tentatively entitled *Ignorant Armies*.

Find I cannot write without endless parenthesis (a parenthesis indicates the simultaneity of past, present and emergent future). I exist in the present moment. I can't and won't pretend I am dead. This novel is not posthumous. A "novel" is something finished, that is, dead—

I am trying, like Klee, *to create something that will have a life of its own, that can put me in real danger, a danger which I willingly take on myself.*

My thoughts turn to crime, incredible journeys of exploration, expression in terms of an *extreme act,* some excess of feeling or behavior that will shatter the human pattern.

Klee expresses a similar idea: "The painter who is called will come near to the secret abyss where elemental law nourishes evolution." And Genet, in his *Journal of a Thief:* "The creator has committed himself to the fearful adventure of taking upon himself, to the very end, the perils risked by his creatures."

Genet says he chose the life of a French thief for the sake of *depth.* By the fact of this depth, which is his greatness, he is more humanly involved than I am. He carries more excess baggage. I only have one "creature" to be concerned with: myself.

Four months ago I took a two-week sleep cure—a ghastly routine. I had it almost made. Another five days sans junk would have seen me in the clear. Then I relapsed. Just before relapse, I dreamed the following:

I was in high mountains covered with snow. It was in a suicide clinic: "You just wait till you feel like it." I was on a ledge with a boy, about sixteen years old—I could feel myself slipping further and further out, out of my *body*, you dig. I don't mean a physical slipping on the ledge. The Plane was coming for me. (Suicide is performed by getting in this Plane with a boy. The Plane crashes in the Pass. No Plane ever gets through.)

Marv reaches out and catches my arm and says: "Stay here with us a while longer."

The suicide clinic is in Turkey. Nothing compulsory. You can leave anytime, even take your boy out with you. (Boat whistle in the distance. A bearded dope fiend rushing to catch the boat for the mainland.) My boy says he won't leave with me unless I kick my habit.

Earlier dream-fantasy: I am in a plane trying to make the Pass. There is a boy with me, and I turn to him and say: "Throw everything out."

"What! All the gold? All the guns? All the junk?"

"Everything."

I mean throw out all excess baggage: anxiety, desire for approval, fear of authority, etc. Strip your psyche to the bare bones of spontaneous process, and you give yourself one chance in a thousand to make the Pass.

I am subject to continual routines, which tear me apart like a homeless curse. I feel myself drifting further and further out, over a bleak dream landscape of snow-covered mountains.

This novel is a scenario for future action in the real world. *Junk, Queer, Yagé*, reconstructed my past. The present novel is an attempt to create my future. In a sense it is a guidebook, a map. The first step in realizing this work is to leave junk forever.

I'll maintain this International Sophistico-criminal Mahatma con no longer. It was more or less shoved on me anyway. So I say: "Throw down all your arms and armor, walk straight to the Frontier."

A guard in a uniform of human skin, black buck jacket with carious yellow tooth buttons, an elastic pullover shirt in burnished Indian copper, adolescent Nordic suntan-brown slacks, sandals from the calloused foot sole of a young Malay farmer, an ash-brown scarf knotted and tucked in the shirt. He is a sharp dresser since he has nothing to do, and saves all his pay, and buys fine clothes and changes three times a day in front of an enormous magnifying mirror. He has a handsome, smooth Latin face with a pencil-line mustache, small brown eyes blank and greedy, eyes that never dream, insect eyes.

When you get to the Frontier, this guard rushes out of his *casita*, where he was plucking at his mustache, a mirror slung round his neck in a wooden frame. He is trying to get the mirror off his neck. This has never happened before, that anyone ever actually got to the Frontier. The guard has injured his larynx taking off the mirror frame. He has lost his voice. He opens his mouth and you can see his tongue jumping around inside. The smooth, blank, young face and the open mouth with the tongue moving inside are incredibly hideous. The guard holds up his hand, his whole body jerking in convulsive negation. I pay no attention to him. I go over and unhook the chain across the road. It falls with a clank of metal on stone. I walk through. The guard stands there in the mist, looking after me. Then he hooks the chain up again and goes back inside the *casita* and starts plucking at his mustache.

At times I feel myself on the point of learning something basic. I have achieved moments of inner silence.

III. WORD

WORD

The Word is divided into units which be all in one piece and should be so taken, but the pieces can be had in any order being tied up back and forth in and out fore and aft like an innaresting sex arrangement. This book spill off the page in all directions, kaleidoscope of vistas, medley of tunes and street noises, farts and riot yipes and the slamming steel shutters of commerce, screams of pain and pathos and screams plain pathic, copulating cats and outraged squawk of the displaced Bull-head, prophetic mutterings of *brujo* in nutmeg trance, snapping necks and screaming mandrakes, sigh of orgasm, heroin silent as the dawn in thirsty cells,

Radio Cairo screaming like a berserk tobacco auction, and flutes of Ramadan fanning the sick junky like a gentle lush worker in the gray subway dawn, feeling with delicate fingers for the green folding crackle.

This is Revelation and Prophecy of what I can pick up without FM on my 1920 crystal set with antennae of jissom. Gentle reader, we see God through our assholes in the flashbulb of orgasm. Through these orifices transmute your body, the way out is the way in. There is no blacker blasphemy than spit with shame on the body God gave you. And woe unto those castrates who equate their horrible old condition with sanctity.

Cardinal———(who shall be a nameless asshole) read *Baby Doll* in the Vatican crapper and shit out his prostate in pathic dismay. "Revolting," he trills. His cock and balls long since dissolve inna thervith of shit death and taxes.

Armed with a meat cleaver, the Author chase a gentle reader down the Midway and into the Hall of Mirrors, trap him impaled on crystal cocks.

With a cry squeezed out by the hanged man's spasm, I raise my cleaver. . . . Will the Governor intervene? Will the whimpering chair be cheated of young ass? Will the rope sing to empty air? Go unused to mold with old jockstraps in the deserted locker room?

The Word, gentle reader, will flay you down to the laughing bones and the author will do a striptease with his own intestines. Let it be. No holes barred. The Word is recommended for children, and convent-trained cunts need it special to learn what every street boy knows: "He who rims the Mother Superior is a success-minded brown nose and God will reward him on TV with a bang at Question 666."

Mr. America, sugar-cured in rotten protoplasm, smiles idiot self bone love, flexes his cancerous muscles, waves his erect cock, bends over to show his asshole to the audience, who reel back blinded by beauty bare as Euclid. He is hanged by reverent Negroes, his neck snaps with a squashed bug sound, cock rises to ejaculate and turn to viscid jelly, spread through the Body in shuddering waves, a monster centipede squirms in his spine. Jelly drops on the Hangman, who runs screaming in black bones. The centipede writhes around the rope and drops free with a broken neck, white juice oozing out.

Ma looks up from knitting a steel-wool jockstrap and says, "That's my boy."

And Pa looks up from the toilet seat where he is reading *The Plastic Age* he keeps stashed in a rubber box down the toilet on invisible string of Cowper gland lubricant—hardest fabric known, beat ramie hands down and cocks up. Some people get it, some don't. A sleeping acquaintance point to my pearl and say, "*¿Eso, qué es?*" ("What's that?" to you nameless assholes don't know Spanish), and I have secrete this orient pearl before a rampant swine not above passing a counterfeit orgasm in my defenseless asshole. It will not laugh a well-greased siege to scorn—heh heh heh—say, "Mother knows best."

A Marine sneering over his flamethrower quells the centipede with jellied gasoline, ignoring the Defense Attorney scream: "Double Jeopardy: My Client . . ."

The Author will spare his gentle readers nothing, but strip himself brother naked. Description? I bugger it. My cock is four and one-half inches and large cocks bring on my xenophobia. . . . "Western influence!" I shriek, confounded by disgusting alterations. "Landsake like I look in the mirror and my cock undergo some awful sorta sea change. . . ." Like all normal citizens, I ejaculate when screwed without helping hand, produce a good crop of jissom, spurt it up to my chin and beyond. I have observed that small hard cocks come quicker slicker and spurtier.

These things were revealed to me in Interzone, where East meets West coming round the other way. In a great apartment house done in Tibetan Colonial, lamsters from the crime of Iowa look out on snowy peaks and groan with Lotus Posture hip-aches. You hooked on Nirvana, brothers, old purple-assed mandrill gibber and piss down your back and eat your ears off. Carry your great meaningless load in hunger and filth and disease, flop against the mud wall like a cut of wrong meat—the Inspector stamp Reject on you with his seal of shit. And the Nationalist white slaver, "Sidi the Lymph," covers his face with scented Kotex and pass by on the other side; and the bearded old Moslem convert from Ottawa, Illinois, seals a coin in the slack hand intoning Koranic platitudes through his Midwest nose. Chinese boys turn in Dad as a rampant junky, and the Japanese boy has rape his honey-face after subdue her with a jack handle, throw the meat into that volcano and roar home in his hot rod to catch the Milton Berle show. And the Javanese fuck himself with a greased banana in a suburb toilet, and Malays catch halitosis from the copywriters and run for the 6:12 with *Amok* trot—the reference, you ignorant asshole, is to the typical trotting gait of the *Amok*. He does not walk, he does not run, he *trots*—and read "How-to" books: *Thank God for My Bang-Utot Attack*, and *On Being a Latah*. See footnote whyncha? So East screams past West on the scenic railway over the midways of Interzone.

And Mother Green grows geraniums in her asshole, and a mandrake spring from Johnny's deserted cock. The Rock and Rollers crack wise with a cyclotron, shit on the great American deck, wipe their ass with Old Glory and turn the Palomar telescope into the Women's Toilet.

"And is there not perhaps something amiss?" says the World, shitting liver, pissing blood and coughing up tripes and roundworms. "—I don't even feel like a human . . . I mean when the poltergeist come down from the attic and shit in the living room, outnumber the haunted ten to one like niggers and Arabs, and their merry pranks are no longer virginal and they turn vicious with adolescence like apes, and with a monarch's voice fart purple havoc. . . .

"Can you deny your purple-assed Döppelganger? This is the time of Witness, when every soul stands with a naked hard-on in the Hall of Mirrors under the meat cleaver of a disgusted God. What a Gawd has to put up with in this business! No, I will *not* hang you. Much too good for you. You abject citizens couldn't raise the libido to commit a sex murder, mute inglorious Robert Christies give me a pain in my curved ass. Now I'll say it again and I'll say it slow . . . I am *curved*. Did you think to flee God in thy souped-up hot rod and play chicken with the Holy Ghost whilst fucking the Virgin Mary up the ass? Generation of Yipers I spew thee out like a reluctant cocksucker won't swallow the load."

"It's rusty," he complains, "I am subject to the botulism." A wise old thug beat the Great Famine nourishing himself on jissom of street boys sleep naked, he absorb that protein rich in all dietary goodness oral or rectal as the case may be, *mutatis mutandis* fore and aft.

The boy wakes up paralyzed from the waist down, and the Mayan priest has pull a trepanning caper and suck the young boy's libido right out of the hypothalamus with an alabaster straw.

"Nothing like a chilled boy on a hot afternoon. . . . Ever get them hot popovers from a burnin' Nigra? Run a red hot rod in and Swedish glögg pour out the nose. . . ."

So glad to have you aboard, reader, but remember there is only one captain of this shit, and back-street drivers will be summarily covered with jissom and exposed to faggots in San Marco. Do not thrust your cock out the train or beckon lewdly with thy piles, nor flush thy beat Benny down the toilet. (Benny is overcoat in anti-quated Times Square argot.) It is forbidden to use the signal rope for frivolous hangings, or to burn Nigras in the washroom before the other passengers have made their toilet. Show Your Culture. Rusty loads subject to carrying charges, plenty of room in the rear, folks, move back into the saloon.

Bloody Mary's First-Aid Manual for Boys: . . . Erections: Apply tight tourniquet at once, open the urethra with a rusty razor blade a whore shave her cunt with it and trim her rag. Inject hot carbolic acid into the scrotum and administer antivenin shot of saltpeter directly into the hypothalamus. If you are caught short without your erection kit, feed a *candiru* up it to suck out the poison. In stubborn and relapsing cases pelvectomy is indicated.

The *candiru* woman with steel-wool pubic hairs receives clients in her little black hut across the river. . . .

The Child Molester has lured a little changeling into a vacant lot. "Now open your mouth and close your eyes and I'll give you a big old hairy surprise."

"And I've news for thee, uncle," she say, soul kissing a *candiru* up his joint.

A cunt undulates out of a snake charmer's basket. Tourist: "He's pulled the teeth of course."

Do I hear a paretic heckler mutter, "Cathtrathon Complekth God damn it?" Well I'd rather be safe than sorry. Almost anything can lurk up a woman's snatch. Why, a Da is subject to be castrated by his unborn daughter, piranha fingerlings with transparent teeth sharp as glass slivers leave you without a cunt to piss in. Safest way to avoid these horrid perils is come over here and shack up with Scylla, treat you right, kid, candy and cigarettes.

The vibrating chair receives the yellow cop killer, burns his piles white as a dead leech.

Death dressed as an admiral hang Billy Budd with his own hands and Judge Lynch sneer, "Dead suns can't witness." But the witness will rise from the concrete of Hudson with a fossil prick to point out the innocent wise guy.

And when the graves start yielding up the dead—Goddammit I pay rent in perpetuity for the old gash, now she rise like Christ in drag.

It's the final gadget, the last of the big-time gimmicks—wires straight into the hypothalamus orgasm center! White nerves spilling out at ear and winking lewdly from corner of the eye, the queen twitch his switch and pant, "Gawd you heat my synapses! Turn me on DaddyOOOOOOOOOOOH!!"

"You cheap bitch! You nausea artist! I wouldn't demean myself to connect your horrible old synapses." So the queen has slink a slug in the pay toilet and blew her top off with an overcharge.

So this is Smiles Benson, your loathsome counselor. You can just tell old Smiles anything, so come on in, kiddies, and let your hair down with a gash and show me all your interesting sores.

Drop your pants, sister, my Mary hides behind the prostate trap with her protoplasm showing, dissolve herself and run out her bloody cunt. Must be careful of the word bloody. Quite thick in England they tell me. Wouldn't want to offend the office manager and he take back the keys to the office shithouse. Always keep it locked so no Sinister Stranger sneak a shit, give all the kids in the office some horrible disease; and old Mr. Anker from Accounting, his arms scarred like a junky from Wassermanns, spray plastic over it before he travail there.

Prostate white as an eye receives the delight massage, shoot it up the spine to the hypothalamus with delicious bone tickles, the spine squeeze the body in spasms of delight and throws its white juice.

Put the orgasm line direct in the hypothalamus socket and we are in business. My line is Total Disability and Termite-Proof Orgasms. It's the American way, folks, if you want a thing done do it yourself first, then mass-reduce anyone stand still for it, anyplace you can find traction. Hanging is an outmoded trip around the world to the Hypothalamus Orgasm Center. England missed the bus. Don't break your neck to get an orgasm, folks. Buy Uncle Lee's portable charge set, turn you on *direct connection*. Shit sure contract your spine in spasms.

"Turn the cocksucker off!! I'm Stoned!!"

Technicians: "Fluid drained out! Hydraulic switch ain't worth a fart." He mixes a bicarbonate of soda and belches into his hand. White bone juice spurt out.

The Jordanian soldier, convict of selling a map of the barracks privy to Jew agents, hanged in the marketplace of Amman, crawl up onto the gallows poop deck to hoist the Black Wind Sock of the Insect Trust. Black rocks and great brown lagoons invade the world silent and sure as junk taking the sick cells.

There stands the deserted transmitter, crystal tubes click on the message of retreat from the Human Hill.

"Fellow worshippers of the Centipede God, there is no halfway house. To compromise at animal level were to invite carnivorous disaster, and as such I protest. We gotta make it all the way lest any citizen raise his voice to say, 'I do not check those deeds that you have done!' "

Only the dry hum of wings rub together and giant centipedes crawl in the ruined city of our long home.

Thermodynamics has won at a crawl. . . . Orgone balked at the post. . . . Christ bled. . . . Time ran out.

"We were caught with our pants down," admits General Peterson. "They rimmed the shit out of us."

Will the centipede stand in the spine like he's supposed? Will Greg let his bone-teasing lover Brad hang him for kicks? He shove his hypothalamus, rotten with stasis sores all over it, into Brad's face and scream, "Break it, Brad, and let the white juice flow! Bury me under the school privy, let the winds of East Texas whimper through my ribs filling up with young boy sweet shit."

The spectators scream through the Track. The electronic brain shivers berserk in blue and pink and chlorophyll orgasms, spitting out money printed on rolls of toilet paper, condoms full of ice cream, Kotex hamburgers—FBI files spurt out in a great blast of bone meal, garden tools and barbecue sets whistle through the air, skewer the spectators. A million jukeboxes truck and jitterbug and waltz and mambo across the floor, snatch money from the spectators, shove it up the slot. A rousing Bronx cheer throws a silent greased spray of glass across the bars and soda fountains and lunch rooms of America and the jukebox goes out like a dead electric eye. Mixmasters attack the markets and fields, orchards and warehouses, flood the world with juice. Bendixes tear clothes from spectators, snap up sheets and rugs. The Brain spews out test results; positive Wassermann ejects a huge rubber spirochete, albuminous urine throws out an artificial kidney, Contraceptive Unit rams a squealing peccary up a woman's snatch with vaginal jelly; the cream separator has cut a cow in half, and the automatic milker jack boys off to white bone juice, carries it away in slop bucket to feed the hogs that never touch the ground, supported in plastic slings, great globs of fat folding over the mouth, like a gorged tick—tiny hooves stick out the white lard wiggling feeble. And the halitosis tester billows out rings of pure black stink, sear the lungs like burning shit, and the electric chair executes at ten-minute intervals equipped with built-in court and jail.

"Just feed your criminal into the machine and his cremated ashes fall out the other end in a plastic Chimu Funeral Urn. Infallible electronic jurisprudence prevent miscarriages and Suburbia is spared screams for mercy or some nausea artist strip on the gallows with a hard-on, scream, 'I'm ready for a meet with my maker!' and leer at the doctor so nasty or roll around the gas chamber floor shitting and ejaculating, while the sheriff whimpers at the witness slot—and who want to see the prick turn red like an old blood sausage and burst open when the switch goes home? The machine does it all, folks."

General Peterson leaps on a Bendix and careens around the track at supersonic speed, his voice falls out of his empty wake of air—"Hold that line, boys! Exterminate the bastards!" He is washed away screaming in a river of DDT.

The thinking machine runs out of thought, and sucks the brains out of everybody with stainless steel needles glittering in pinball pinks and gas flares and sky rockets.

Outside, the dry husk of insects. . . .

Now the thoughtful reader may have observed certain tendencies in the author might be termed unwholesome. In fact some of you may be taken aback by the practices of this character. The analyst say: "Mr. Lee have you not consider, to thread thy cock on a lifelong oyster string of pearly cunts and get with normal suburban kicks is chic as Cecil Beaton's ass this season in Hell?"

I call in my friends and we spend whole evenings listen to the Bendix sing "Sweet and Low," "The Wash Machine Boogie"; and the sinister cream separator, a living fossil, bitter as rancid yak butter, seeks the bellowing Hoover with a leopard's grunt. Suburbia hath horrors to sate a thousand castrates and stem the topless cocks of Israel.

Going my way, brother? The hitchhiker walks home through gathering mushroom clouds, and we meet in the Dead Ass Café, to break glass ashtrays over our foreheads pulsing in code . . . slip with a broken neck to the ground-floor mezzanine and put sickness up the cunt of Mary, yearly wounded with a frightened girl.

Brothers, the limit is not yet. I will blow my fuse and blast my brains with a black short-circuit of arteries, but I will not be silent nor hold longer back the enema of my word hoard, been dissolving all the shit up there man and boy forty-three years and who ever held an enema longer? I claim the record, folks, and any Johnny-Come-Late think he can out-nausea the Maestro, let him shove his ass forward and do a temple dance with his piles.

"Not bad, young man, not bad. But you must learn the meaning of discipline. Now you will observe in my production every word got some kinda awful function fit into mosaic on the shithouse wall of the world. That's discipline, son. Always at all times know thy wants and demand same like a thousand junkies storm the crystal spine clinics cook down the Gray Ladies."

The bartender has kick the Sellubi, his foot sink in the ass and the Sellubi comes across the dusty floor. The bartender braces himself against the brass rail, put other foot in the Sellubi's back and pops him off into the street.

"Step right up ladies and gents to see this character at the risk of all his appendages and extremities and appurtenances will positively shoot himself out of a monster asshole. . . ." An outhouse is carried in on the shoulders of Southern Negroes in dungarees, singing spirituals.

"And the walls come tumbling down."

The outhouse falls in a cloud of powdered wood and termites, and the Human Projectile stands there in his black shit suit. A giant rubber asshole in a limestone cliff clicks open and sucks the Human Projectile in like spaghetti. Noise of distant thunder and the Projectile pops out with a great fart, flies a hundred feet through the air into a net supported by four gliders. His shit suit splits and a round worm emerges and does a belly dance. The worm suit peels off like a condom and the Aztec Youth stands naked with a hard-on in the rising sun, ejaculates bloody crystals with a scream of agony. The crowd moans and whimpers and writhes. They snatch up the stones dissolve in red and crystal light. . . . The boy has gone away through an invisible door.

Nimun with sullen cat eyes look for a scrap of advantage, he snap it up and carry it away to the secret place where he lives and no one can find the way to his place. Old queens claw wildly at his bronze body, scream, "Show me your secret place, Nimun. I'll give you all my hoard of rotten ectoplasm."

"What place? You dreaming, mister? I live in the Mills Hotel."

"But WHERE YOU BEEN??????????"

The Skip Tracer has come to disconnect your hypothalamus for the nonpayment of orgones:

"I got a fact process here, Jack. You haven't paid your orgone bill since you was born already and used to squeak out of the womb, 'Don't pay it Ma. Think of your unborn child. You wanta get the best for me,' like a concealed rat. Know this, Operators, Black and Gray Marketeers, Pimps and White Slavers, Paper Hangers of the world: no man can con the Skip Tracer when he knocks on your door with a fact process. He who gives out no orgones will be disconnected from life for the nonpayment."

"But give me time. I'm caught short. . . ."

"Time ran out in the 5th at Tropical. . . . Disconnect him boys."

"Lost my shoe up him," grumbles the bartender. "My feet are killing me, I got this condition of bunions you wouldn't believe it. Turn on the ventilator, Mike. When a man live on other people's shit he can fart out a stink won't quit. I knew this one Sellubi could fart out smoke rings, and they is bad to shoplift with their prehensile piles. . . ."

"Order in the court! You are accused of soliciting with prehensile piles. What have you to say in your defense?"

"Just cooling them off, Judge. Raw and bleeding . . . wouldn't you?"

Judge: "That's beside the point. . . . What do you recommend, Doctor?"

Dr. Burger: "I recommend hypothalamectomy."

The Sellubi turns white as a dead leech and shits his blood out in one solid clot. Warm spring rain washes shit off a limestone statue of a life-size boy hitchhiking with his cock. "GOING MY WAY?" in dead neon on a red-brick dais overlook a deserted park in East St. Louis.

The Hoover bellows retreat and the Business Man says to his honey-face, "I'm tired, sweet thing, and got the rag on."

The team hangs Brad in the locker room. Ceremonial dress of shoulder pads and jockstrap. His friend will pull the jockstrap down, let the cock spurt free and break his neck with a stiff arm. He is buried under the school outhouse where black widows lurk is bad to bite young boy ass.

Fearless boy angels fly through the locker room jacking off, "Whooooooooooooooooo"—they jet away in white wake of jissom, leave a crystal laugh hang in the air.

Transmute your substance. . . . Burn the black shit blue. No disgust on the human tightrope. Stay on that rope brothers and sisters and those who evade the sex census holed up in the mountains of Interzone.

No one transmute by proxy, nor send the chauffeur with thy pelvis in a hat box, nor Nubian Expeditor bearing your hypothalamus in a crystal cylinder. Folks, you must bring your own ass in at the door. The Saint can't come for you and why should I repeat myself in your horrible old body disgust me already with stasis sores?

Negroes with sad monkey eyes stand in a jungle clearing— animal substance invades the thickening face—disease of the race in blood and bones, and white lymphogranuloma swell the groins. Little toe amputates spontaneous, it's a dirty nigger trick, and the bleached-blond-passing replica crook her little toe elegant, it drop off clean and bloodless on Mrs. Worldly's drawing-room floor.

Great raindrops fall like crystal skulls through the green air, and Portuguese gauchos with huge black mustaches ride through the clearing, sing strange sad songs. Planters use cured Nigra balls on the golf course, whacking them over the gallows. Their women sit on the club veranda. Peeled balls float like opal chips in jars of glycerin at withered yellow necks, a resplendent tiara at the governor's ball catch the Aladdin lamp sputter of burning insect wings. The woman dreams of a Black Mamba and wake shrieking, "The houseboy fucked me!"

"Rusty load of ectoplasm . . . gotta score for a medium tonight," said the arty ghost. "Don't have a regular stand like some lucky pricks go around all the time on the nod. Earth-bound to the monkey three hundred years man boy and ghost."

Spontaneous amputation of cock occurs among boys, it just turn to shit and pop off with a fart. The boy picks his cock out of shit shale, the careful archaeologist, and sprays shellac all over it—subject to turn to dust when it hits the air after all those shit-bound years.

Johnny make it all the way in St. Louis before spellbound audience—throw off his pink bathrobe naked as the Young Corn God, hang himself for keeps ejaculating crystal skulls. . . . There was this citizen have a circus act, hang himself with a special elastic rope. A dangerous act they tell me, you gotta check the rope for elasticity before every performance. In St. Louis he didn't check the rope and his neck snapped, he was carried out by leering cops with a paralyzed hard-on . . . and the last spasm on the operating table under floodlight—a trouper to the end. The wind sock sags and the croaker shakes his head and the nurse covers Johnny's prick with a sheet.

So he turns to limestone, and setting his hard cock in the cunt of shadow, fades down the mountainside, and pipes call "Taps for Danny Boy" and "Johnny's So Long at the Fair."

The Ringmaster has pulled a rope switch . . . the old army game. "The One, the Only, Midway Johnny, though his spine breaks in his neck, gives the performance of all time!"

The Dreamer—impresario of that Los Angeles cemetery underlines mortality with shit—gilds Johnny with angel wings springing from an outhouse on the tomb of a rich old queen rolls right over in her grave.

"Just build a privy over me, boys," said the rustler to his bunk-mates, and the sheriff nods in dark understanding. Druid blood stirring in the winds of Panhandle, and bloody rites to the Cow God are consummate in the Sacred Cottonwood groves. Johnny is eaten in Kansas City by bankers and brokers with black mustache and gold watch chain.

"Now that's what I call *tenderloin*," B.Q. says, pensively studying a sliver of red meat on the end of his toothpick.

"Yeah, but the meat's gotta *hang*. . . . Now in Dodge City they are serving raw unparalyzed boys is subject to come up on a poor old queen and slice her motherfucking head off and rummage through her intestines for gold fillings. Eager beaver might swallow a gold crown with the jissom."

"But here the boys is cut down to eating size the way I like to see a cut of boy, Clem."

The Cow God and the Horse God, the Bank God, the Cop God and the Eunuch God of Small Business claim their yearly crop of Young Gods in the Vibrating Chair, the Green Outhouse and the rope sing like wind in wire.

And the broker shits Johnny out in his marble shithouse with sunken bath, smokes his great greasy Havana, chewing it slow and dirty, and take the chewed end out to look at and lick his mustache and belch.

Lean sick junkies play Banker and Broker in Washington Square.

"Billy Budd must hang! All hands aft to see this exhibit." Billy Budd gives up the ghost with a great fart, and the sail is rent from top to bottom, and the petty officers fall back confounded. . . . "Billy" is a transvestite Liz. "There'll be a spot of bother about this," mutters the Master-at-Arms, breathing into his halitosis tester.

The tars scream with rage at the cheating profile in the rising sun. The Liz gives a few tired old kicks and throws a little sliver of black shit curved like a pigtail.

"Is she dead?"

"So who cares?"

"Are we going to stand still for this, boys? The officers pull a switch on us," said young Hassan, Ship's Uncle.

"Gentlemen," said Captain Vere, "I cannot find words to castigate this foul and unnatural act whereby a boy's mother take over his body, infiltrate her horrible old substance right onto a decent boat and, with bare tits hanging out, unfurl the nastiest colors of the spectroscope."

All the world's a gallows and we all play with our parts, some are towel boys, others lewd doctors, most of us just dirty old men whimper at life's Glory Hole.

A young kid has wandered in off the range with the winds of Texas in his hair. He wipes his ass pensively with a Mandrake.

A great black tornado has sucked meaning from the Cyclone Belt. Citizens crawl out of the cellar in a blighted subdivision, look after the cyclone with canceled castrate eyes. . . .

"Lawd! Lawd! I don't even feel like a human."

"At least the TV is left."

They squeak out a feeble "Hallelujah."

See, the sheriff frame every good-looking kid in the country, say, "Guess I'll have to hang some cunt for the new *frisson*. He hang this cute little corn-fed thing, her tits come to attention, squirt milk in his eye blind him like a spitting cobra.

"Oh land's sake!" say the sheriff. "I shoulda never hang a woman. A man can only come off a second best he tangle assholes with a gash. Well, I guess I can see with my mouth from here on in. Hehe hehe heh."

So the sheriff have glass eyes made up with filthy pictures built in—her is walking penny arcade—and feel the kid up, and that hot blood hit the young cock, and the kid's breath get short, and the sheriff's steady finger (best shot in Dead Coon County) unbutton his fly slow and just ease the cock out stand up there pulsing in the Old Privy all overgrown with weeds and vines, rusty smell of shit turning back to soil.

Come in at the door after delouse treatment. Don't give halo lice to your fellow angels. They will sneer at you and hamstring your harp.

"You want to lose that proboscis?" she say. Her cunt click open like a snap-knife.

Don't offend with innocence. Need Life Boy soap. Body smell of life a nasty odor in the snooze of a decent American gash.

See this Liz fuck a kid with a April Fool exploding prick, and it go off inside and blow his guts right outa navel. The Liz roll on the floor laughing, yell, "Oh! Oh! Give me ribs of steel."

Any woman get gay with me after all I suffer from the fairy-making sex bite off more than she can chew, even with my lymphogranuloma I can still kick shit out of Brubeck the Unsteady lose his in the thervith of junk and the slunk traffic.

"The gimmick is this, Doc: tell a farmer his cow give birth to a monster and you had to burn it already, goosed by your Veterinary Ethics. We can't miss."

. . . It's the only way to live . . . a few chickens . . . jug of paregoric and thou under the swamp cypress. Sweet screams of burning Nigra drift in on the warm spring wind fans our hot bodies like a Nubian slave. How obliging can you get?

The boy trots along the curb with tireless *amok* trot of the Indian-giver to a perilous scaffold of rusty iron, termite-eaten wood, rotten rope. Meets a young junky—black hair uncombed, black eyes with pinpoint green pupils open on the Green Death Room (one reference, gentle reader, is to the Green Room in San Quentin where cyanide executions are consummated under civil leers of the witnesses).

Papers of heroin stashed in the history book, he fixes in the school toilet. Narcotics agent, peeping through the glory hole, has caught a kid in the junk act, slaps the cuffs on his ankles.

I ask the boy how old he is and he say, "I'm seventeen."

I nod with dark understanding and say, "Junkies always look younger than they are."

"How they hangin', Herman?" Old fat junky cheat on his rope with cyanide.

It's the Plastic Age, folks. 'Tain't no sin take off your new skin and clown around in your bone-ons.

That good Black Gum with hot Arab tea hits you ten minutes like a ton of shit. . . . Black Death Terry called his Ford the river of sticks to Reynosa Boy's Town where the mangy lioness was to break his neck with one quick claw. . . . That's what happen when you wake a sleeping lioness with the flashbulb of urgency. She don't like it. And the Chinaman don't like it. Don't ever wake that Chinaman with a heroin flash.

(Young friend of mine name of Terry have this 1936 Ford he call the Black Death. One night he get in the Black Death and cross the Rio Grande to Reynosa, where a mangy old lioness stood in a cage in Joe's patio. So Terry goes in the cage, throw a flashlight in the lioness' face, who leap on him and break his neck, and the bartender vault over the bar with a forty-five blast the lioness. But Mr. Terry he dead.)

The blond woman came in through the white door with a holly wreath on it, and took down my wine-colored pants. Drank champagne from the living cunt with breakfast sausage and scrambled eggs.

Where you been? This young cat eat sausages out of a woman's cunt (prominent actress) at a Berlin party in Weimar days. Later he run into this same cunt fully dressed at another party and say, "*Wie gehts?*" or something . . . and she draw herself up and sneer: "Where is your culture, you nameless asshole? I don't know you."

And he says, "But Fräulein, I have et the blood sausage from your cunt at Mitzi's Comming-off and Going-away Party."

And she says, "Oh dahling! . . . Of course! Mitzi's such an old castrate." Such was life in the Weimar Republic.

Boy on the way to Lexington jacks off in the shuddering junk-sick toilet. Girls scream by on the scenic railway over the edge of space into the night. . . . "Put out your condom, kid, and Santa drop a cunt in it."

So I say to this broad, I say, "Listen baby you ought to take a picture. Do you dye your cunt or shave it?"

The Caid in gasoline screams up the Midway to the burning roller coaster where the boy stood on the heroin deck proclaiming his habit to the sneers of sick physicians.

The trap falls with tremendous speed, no time for breakfast. Let it come down and fix the black bone yen.

Burning high yeller boy tied to a packing crate with barbed wire at wrist and ankle, screams out of his flesh and runs across the red clay of Georgia in black bones.

London Bridge is falling, slow trap through the long white nerves and green intestine jungles and the pearly glands. . . . Slow fall. . . .

In the Closed Garden the Boy runs in a curved fold, pants of Nexus burn with jellied Narcissism—incandescent pelvis among the geraniums. . . . Outside yipping Arabs barbecue sad-eyed Indians in pink Cadillacs.

Junk yacks at our heels a silent riot, and predated checks bounce all around us like fossil skulls in a Mayan ball court.

"Dicks scream for dope fiend lover"—A savage spot haunted by a woman scream for her demon lover, Coleridge, "Xanadu"— another old-time schmecker.

Dead bird, quail in the slipper, money in the bank. Fossil cunts of predated chicks bounce around us in Queens Plaza. Lay them in the crapper—just shove it in, vibration does the rest. Old stove burn nostalgia, and black dust rain down over us cancer curse of switch. Cock under the nut shell.

"Step right up. Now you see it, now you don't."

The penis is not of mine to give is passport of cunt. Past port and petal crowned with calm leaves she stand there across the river under the trees.

"Come," she says. "Come, and you can suck my marshmallows, and I will show my little black box of Turkish Exquisitries." (.32 prick cover this caper, penis in hand.)

(Proprietor of a Turkish Exquisitries shop shot by holdup man with .32.)

The light shakes over the lake, and the wild cataract leaps through the Glory Hole, blinding the old queen in the next cavity. Spitting cobras, patronize your neighborhood toilet.

Adolescent angels sing on shithouse walls of the world: "Come and Jack Off . . . 1929." "Gimpy pushes milk sugar shit . . . Johnny Hung Lately, 1952." Deserted farm outhouse (shit turn back dust to dust).

Telegram from your boy buried under the outhouse forty-year shit strata . . . sing over the deep river into K-Y Inferno (female impersonator joint).

"I got the calling," scream the female impersonator like a horse kicked in the nuts. Orient Express screaming train whistle, and the chic young agent summarily hanged at the Turkish border for possession of Exquisitries turns out to be female impersonator from Yokohama with a strap-on cunt fly off in last orgasm. Bullfighter's cap caught by The Witness . . . hiatus of time out when the banana slip up his ass, goose him onto the long horn.

Come in at the Door Jam. Don't worry about a Thing Man. Where'd you get it? Shaking that thing. The prostate back trap door let it down, shit out the marines like a landing barge, nail it shut with cobwebs.

Frontier moves out into space-time—phantom riders, chili joints, saloon and the Quick Draw, hangings from horseback to the jeers of Sporting Women. Black Smoke on the hip in the Chinese Laundry. . . . No tickee, no washee. Clom Fliday.

Chinese pushers stopped serving Occidentals in the 1920s. When a junky want to score off the Chink, he say, "No glot. Come Fliday."

Golden horses copulate in black clouds of West.

The quaint English gangster is in the marl hole of the world.

In front of the mutilated limestone fragments of museum, Indian boys with bright red gums are eating the green ices.

Mr. Gilly looks for his brindle-faced cow across the Piney Woods where armadillos innocent of a cortex frolic under the .22 of black Stetson and pale blue eyes.

When the author was raising marijuana in East Texas, he unwillingly made the acquaintance of one Mr. Gilly, a rural mooch leave low pressure area in his wake like an impotent cyclone, toothless snarl of blackmail, weak and intermittent like music down a windy street. "Lawd Lawd, have you seen my brindle-faced cow? Guess I'm taking up too much of your time. Must be busy doing *something*, feller say. Good stand you got, whatever it is. Maybe I'm asking too many questions. Weell, guess I'll be getting along. You wouldn't have a rope, would you? A *hemp* rope? Don't know how I'd hold that old brindle-faced cow without a rope if I did come on him. No, I guess not. Well, now you got that new Chevy, I guess you'd most *give* your old jeep to a poor man. You wouldn't have a cold drink, would you?"

In England are bottomless holes used as public tips (dumps), known as marl holes, where English gangsters dump copper's narks in oil tins—until the busies put a watchman on the hole to prevent such violations of the sanitary code.

The museum at Guatemala City, looted by Mayan collectors of the world, has left a few old beat-up pieces of stelae. Set in a little park grove of trees.

Money all over him like shit you can smell it. And Rocky smell so sweet of junk always leave that selfish smell never come off a man handle it, use it, junk cling to him like jellied ectoplasm, burns out whiffs of black smoke.

The Operator want to suck the emergent maleness of the passing queen . . . wise prick know when the bones will change and jump on that wagon break its ass with his weight of centuries, sit and take his cut and never never give nothing back. Got the Big Fix up his ass in a finger stall with 14-carat diamonds, antibiotics and heroin. Under Corn Hole Sign of carny lot caretaker toolshed.

"Drop your pants, kid." Over the broken chair and out through the dusty window—Midway boarded up for winter, whitewash whip in a cold wind on limestone cliff over the river—pieces of moon hang like smoke in the cold blue substance of sky out on a long line of jissom spurt across the dusty floor.

"See you Joe's Lunch. Treat you meal. What'll you have, kid? Two chilis with cherry crumb pie and white coffee."

"Like this," he say on all fours, cup the boy's tits with hard palms, shove it in with a slow sideways wiggle, pull the boy's body on to him with long strokes sculpt stomach, arch like a cat pulling up into his stomach, up and in.

Balls squeezed dry black lemon rind pest rim the ass with a knife cut off piece of hash for the water pipe bubble tube indicate what used to be me.

"The river is served, sir."

In the barn attic came on the wetback sleep with hard-on under thick cotton pants . . . sits up with fierce eyes, smile sweet, bright red gums, look down and stretch his body, and I reach slow and touch it. He sit me down and make the strip motion, and I undo belt silent and shaking and shove my pants down slow. Cock spring out hard, turn me around, sink slow fence post in hole, quicksand, rubber boots slow in, the boy shudder and sigh. Black widow fall on the wetback's copper neck, bite him; die in quick convulsions allergic shock—come five times.

The young rustler say to his friend, "You do it." And the friend take the noose, looking into his friend's eyes, put it over his head and adjust behind the left ear—ritual gentleness of sacrifice. "You'd better stand up in the saddle." Help him up with tied hands, leaning against his friend's hard young body keep him from falling on the hemp (premature ejaculation unhealthy practice the experts say). Stand now like a young god ready: "Well, go ahead, Greg." They stand there, one steadying the other with hand on his shoulder, young males gentle and sad, and the wind ripples through their hair in a vibrating soundless hum under the cottonwoods. The two boys change middle-aged hennaed fags, start back from each other appalled by the hideous sea change, and Johnny falls from the saddle. Mandrakes pop up with pathic screams.

Crawl out and identify yourselves before we throw in a Mills Brothers cough drop or a chocolate éclair, and the third time he go down for the long count tangled in seaweed, down there looking for his fish dinner.

"Let's shake the joint down." Freudian dicks burst in like burning lions.

"Ground floor dining room, so-called living room, den, kitchen, pantry, toilet under the stairs."

"We been over this a million times. Really, Doctor, if you have nothing further to enlighten us, shut your doddering mouth whyncha?"

"Second floor."

"Don't make with the room layout again, or I shall scream."

"Toilet lead right into our lady's dressing room soft silky smells perfume and cold cream and whiff of diarrhea shit smell yellow, the way old three-day vintage smell black. Ever whiff green shit? A sort of shiny green-black glows in the dark? But that was in another country, and besides—"

"Shut up already, murder never outlaws. The fuzz try hanging this meatball rap on me as notorious Blue Ball and Torso Artist."

"Never outlaws." I.e., the statute of limitations does not run. Blue balls are a symptom of real evil clap.

The arrow right through his eye and out the back of that adorable head. Shrunk down I keep it up my ass in a plastic cover on a long gold chain. Lovely mouth falls open as if petulant wake from sleep with a sulky hard-on, he dead falls with a soft plop in the Amazon mud.

"Well," she says, "I got this vibrator off my cousin Fred connect with the black market for these coupons entitle him all different gadgets—folding bidet carry up your ass, open out like an umbrella. And the handbag cream separator, second as weapon a girl caught short-armed with a prick up her."

Long line of black boys march up the ramp to the hidden gallows singing spirituals. And when they open the door underneath cut them down with a Kansas combo the warm wheaty odor of semen drifts out across the blighted continent, South of the Border, wanders in miasmal mists and ambrosial fogs flowers in a clear green switch.

Jim goose Brad, say "Ooooooooooh," and his teeth pop out with a fart into the clear blue mountain lake, turn into a lamprey and swim away to suck a silver trout.

The face strangles (audience gags and stick out tongues), veins pop in the brain like little red firecrackers, blue sparks fly from broken connections, lights go off in square blocks of power failure. Light across Long Island park and trees in the bright sun seen from the El shake through the young body. (America a great plain under the wings of vultures husk in the dry air.)

Cool as blue-eyed young junky spectral in the sun. Hot as blood leap to mouth and cock, and the eyes go black and blood sing in the ears sweet as little pink conchs.

"The question is this," said the philosophic doctor, that old tired prop him up, downing a mason jar of corn. "Can the pleasure of a sex act, deeply repressed say like MacArthur we have returned and squeeze out the jet at tremendous pressure, be qualitatively more intense than the normally charged act?"

Blast of trumpets, drool of drums and dead march. And decayed corseted tenor sings "Danny Deever" in drag: "They have taken all his buttons off and cut his pants away. Bastard browned the colonel sleeping, the man's ass is all agley. And he'll swing in harf a minute for a sneaking, shooting fay. They are 'angin' Danny Deever in the morning."

Lights: a stage stretching to the neon skyline. Golden gallows towers a thousand feet against the Grand Canyon, Pikes Peak, Niagara Falls and Chrysler Building, vast souvenir postcards light up slow with neon.

Motel. Motel. Motel loneliness moans across the continent like foghorns over still oily waters of tidal rivers. Violet's Massage Parlour in green neon. The Girl in White greases up a vibrator. The boy watches her face black down to a little green dot.

Hanging togs at Antoine's, emporium for young fags of good family. We have literally thousands of escape suits for the—tee hee—bride.

"May I kiss the bride?"

The skull nods knowingly. Antoine claps imperious hands, and the Fashion Show is on.

Boy drops on a blue rope. Blue flame burns round his waist,

and his pants fall free, burning, into a dark lagoon in the empty park. Shirt burns in blue flare light his grinding bone grins. The separate spine squeeze the soft body up and out the cock.

Escape suit burn blue all over, cook the boy while he come, spit hot balls out his cock. (Negro smile malevolently, catch them on a skewer. "Hot balls, folks! Hot balls!" He moves up through the aisles. Circus, Stadium, Plaza.)

Our Snow Drop Suit guaranteed to liquefy. We have never had a failure. When you shoot that rusty dark load cross the night like a shooting star.

Cowboy suit dissolves in a mist of powder smoke, clear to show bunkmate reverently pull off the boots . . . and with beatified face receive the benediction of sperm sweet as warm summer rain on the face and hair.

The Preaching Hangman touches the boy's neck with hands, sweet slime like a snail. "Now, ladies and gentles of this congregation. When I hang a man and think of his lluuuuuvelay soul bear his rusty load right up God's ass—how old did you say, sheriff?"

"Sixteen."

"Looks younger. —Sometimes I really haaaaate this job." He wipes the foam from his lips with an eiderdown.

Soldier suit dissolve, run down the body. Our permanent plating process guarantee you an interested niche in any park, hang off the limp foot in a bronze tear.

Suits turn to shit and drip off you swung out over the privies of the world on a long black bolo. Angel suits made of marshmallows and spun sugar sweet burn, leave the little naked boy twitching. (Sweet young breath quick through the teeth, stomach hard as marble spits it out in soft sweet blobs. Spurty boy comes, slower and slower and slower turn to a long yellow beard in the old man's hands.)

Socially conscious Negroes hang themselves over a fire of packing crates singing "Strange Fruit" slow and fruity, while serious Negroes with rimless glasses and fat smooth coffee faces hand out bills among the audience, well-dressed and vaguely embarrassed. (Whiff of dried jissom in a bandanna rises out of a hotel drawer, ghost town twenty years shut down, covered with dust.)

"Interesting, don't you think?"

"Decidedly," says the venomous thin-faced Colonel, circumcises a boy with his cigar cutter, lights his cigar with the foreskin.

The boy like a nun so pure and alive for the moment to take the death vow it hurts, a soft blue blast of sadness. Boy grin dissolves slow into the sunlight over the bullhead hole, quarry, vacant lot with a pond in it. The boy looks down at his bloody arms marked with the needle-wound stigmata. Soft sadness of death. Riddled child cancer. "Hope to God the President's Radium Bicycle gets here on time," says the White House Press Department, looking nervously at his watch.

Mirror suits scatter into white sand desert, reveal the vicious leer of the brazen victim.

The hangman in doublet is adjusting the knot with bestial leers and obscene gestures.

A pig forty feet high is sliced open by a huge neon-tube knife. Amusement park stretch in roller-coastering black lace to the horizons of smoky cities.

Greg sits in the school toilet. Clean sharp turds fall out his tight young ass (turds like yellow clay washed clean in summer rain covered with crystal snail tracks in the morning sun lights the green flame of grass).

The man with black Japanese mustache, each hair frozen in white grease. (Black branches with the white ice cover catch the morning sun over a frozen lake when we get back from the hunting trip.)

Ambivalent alcoholic hangs himself with a great Bronx cheer, blasting out all his teeth, and tears at the noose. (Shivering dog breaks his teeth on the steel trap under a cold white moon.)

"Candy, I Call My Sugar Candy." Hanged boy descends on a rope of toffee, comes in the mouth of a fourteen-year-old girl eats toffee and taps out "Candy" on the neon-lighted table—outside, the blight of Oklahoma beaten by the calm young eyes.

The boy has found the vibrator in his mother's closet. They won't be back before five . . . plenty of time. Drops pants to ankles, cock springs up hard and free with that lovely flip make old queen bones stir with root nerves and ligaments. He grease the tip, and it turn into a vulgar cock given to Bronx cheers at moment of orgasm and other shocking departures from good taste. (Emily Post is writing a million-word P.S. to *Etiquette*, entitled *The Cock in Our House*.) He stands front mirror, stick it slow up his ass to the glad gland give a little fart of pleasure. Bubble filled with fart gas hang in the air heavy as ectoplasm dispersed by the winds of morning sweep the dust out with slow old man hands coughing and spitting in the white blast of dawn. Sperm splash the mirror, turn black and go out in a short circuit with ozone smell of burning iron.

Greg has come up behind Brad in the park, goose him and his hand sink in.

"Hello, Brad." He pulls his hand out with a resounding fart and rubs ambergris over his body, poses for *Health and Strength* in faggot-skin jockstrap.

So there he stand on top of the filing cabinet naked as a prick hang out in the muted blue incense of the lesbian temple. (Cold-eyed nuns rustle by, metallic purity leaves a whiff of ozone.) Funny how a man comes back to something he left behind in a Peoria hotel drawer 1932.

You are nearing the frontier where all the pitchmen and street peddlers, three-card-monte quick-con artists of the world spread out their goods. Old pushers, embittered by years of failure, mutter through the endless gray lanes of junk *amok* with a joint (i.e., a syringe), shooting the passersby. The tourist is torn in pieces by Soul Short-Change hypes fight over pieces. (Piranha fish tear each other to great ribbons of black-market beef. White bone glistens through, covered with iridescent ligaments.)

Neon tubes glow in the blood of the world. Everyone see his neighbor clear as an old message on the shithouse wall stand out in white flames of a burning city.

Greg turns away with a cry of defeat. Bone ache for the Marble God smiling into park covered with weeds.

Fish thrown to the seal by naked boy grin for ooze in verdigris: KEEP THE CHANGE.

Smile sweet as a blast of ozone from a June subway, teeth tinkle like little porcelain balls.

Hold your tight nuts frozen in limestone convolutions.

"I'll be right over stick a greased peccary up her Hairy Ear." Albanian argot for cunt.

Sea of frozen shit in the morning sun and maggots twelve feet long stir underneath, the crust breaks here and there. Asshole farts up sulfur gases and black boiling mud.

Crisp green lettuce heads glitter with frost under a tinkling crystal moon.

"We'll make a heap of money, Clem, if the price is right." He plucks a boy's balls, look over careful for lettuce blight, probing veins and ligaments with gentle old-woman fingers, feel soft for the vein in the pink dawn light; and the young boy wake naked out of wet dream, watch his cock spurt into the morning.

The boy flies screaming in a jet of black blood, turns a red tube in the air, ineffable throbbing pink, rains soft pink cushions on your ass in a soft slow come.

The boy has cut off his limestone balls and tossed them to you with a grin—light on water. Now the body sinks with a slow Bronx cheer to a torn pink balloon hang on rusty nail in the barn. Pink and purple lights play over it from a great black crane swing over rubbish heap go back to stone and trees.

His neck has grown around the rope like a tree. (Vine root in old stone wall. Voice fade to decay, loose a soundless puff of dust, fall slow through the sunlight.)

The boy has eaten a pat of butter, turns into middle-aged cardiac. "That's the way I like to see them," says Doctor Dodo Rindfest— known as Doodles to his many friends. "Them old cardiac rams alla time die up a reluctant ewe."

The old queen wallows in bathtub of boy balls. Others jack off over him jitterbugging, walking through the Piney Woods with a .22 in the summer dawn (chiggers pinpoint the boy's groin in red dots), hanging on the back of freight trains career down the three-mile grade into a cowboy ballad bellowed out by idiot cows through the honky-tonks of Panhandle.

Screaming round the roller coaster in a stolen car, play chicken with a bronze scorpion big as a trailer truck on route 666 between Lynchburg and Danville.

The boy rise in sea-green marble to jack off on the stones of Venice invisible to the ravening castrates of the world, fill the canals with miasmic mist of whimpering halitosis can't get close enough to offend.

The boy has hit you with soft snowballs burst in light burn you soft and pink and cold as cocaine.

Don't walk out on a poor old queen leave her paralyzed come to an empty house. Spurt into the cold spring wind whip the white wash in Chicago, into the sizzling white desert, into the limestone quarry, into the old swimming hole, bait a boy's hook for a throbbing sunfish burn the black water with light.

The wind sighs through the silk stocking hang in clear blue of Mexico clear against the mountain a wind sock of sweet life. (Sweet smell of boy balls and rusty iron cool in the mouth.)

Attic under the round window eye. Summer dawn the two young bodies glow incandescent pink copulations, cock sink into the brown pink asshole up the pearly prostate, sing out along the white nerves. First soft licks of rimming tighten balls off like a winch up the ass. Rim on, MacDuff, till the pool be drained and fill with dead brown leaves, dirty snow drift across my body frozen in the kiss wakes the soft purple flower of shit.

The boy burglar fucked in the long jail with the Porter Tuck— a bullfighter of my acquaintance recently gored in the right lung— in the lungs risk the Great Divide, ousted from the cemetery for the nonpayment come gibbering into the queer bar with a mouldy pawn ticket to pick up the back balls of Tent City, where castrate salesmen sing the IBM song in quavering falsetto.

Balls on the window ledge fall like a broken flowerpot onto the pavement of arson yearly wounded to the sea.

Slow cunt tease refuse until the conversion of the Jew to Diesel go around raping decent cars with a nasty old Diesel Conversion Unit cancerous, so red the rosette, on earth as in heaven this day our breadfruit of cunt.

Crabs frolic through his forest, wrestling with the angle hard-on all night thrown in the home full of valor by adolescent rustler, hide in the capacious skirts of home on the range and the hunter come home from the Venus Hill take the back road to the rusty limestone cave.

Rock and roll around the floor scream for junk fix the Black Yen ejaculate over the salt marshes where nothing grow, not even a mandrake. (Year of the rindpest. Everything died, even the hyenas had to bite a man's balls and run like smash and grab.)

Talk long enough say *something*. It's the law of averages . . . a few chickens . . . only way to live.

Don't neglect the fire extinguisher and stand by with the Kotex in case one of these Southern belles get hot and burst into flame. (Bronx cheer of a fire-eater.)

Cleave fast to mayhem and let not arson be far from thee and clamp murder to thy breast with WHOOOOOOOOPS of seal leap at your throat in Ralph's. Not a bit alarmed about that. Think of something else.

We are prepared to divulge all and to state that on a Thursday in the month of September 1917, we did, in the garage of the latter, at his solicitations and connivance, endeavor to suck the cock of one George Brune Brubeck, the Bear's Ass, which act disgust me like I try to bite it off and he slap me and curse and blaspheme like Christopher Marlowe with the shiv through his eye the way it wasn't fitting a larval fag should hear any old nameless asshole unlock his rusty word hoard.

The blame for this atrociously incomplete act rest solidly on the basement of Brubeck, my own innocence of any but the most pure reflex move of self-defense and -respect to eliminate this strange serpent thrust so into my face at risk of my Man Life, so I, not being armed (unfortunately) with a blunderbuss, had recourse to nature's little white soldiers—our brave defenders by land—and bite his ugly old cock in a laudable attempt to circumcise him thereby reduce to a sanitary condition. He, not understanding the purity of my motives, did inopportunely resist my well-meaning would-be surgical intervention, which occasioned to him light contusions of a frivolous nature. Whereupon he did loose upon my innocent head a blast of blasphemies like burning lions or unsuccessful horse abortionists cooked in slow Lux to prevent the shrinkage of their worm.

We are not unaware of the needs of our constituents. Never out of our mind, and you may rest assured that we will leave no turd interred to elucidate these rancid oil scandals. We will not be intimidated by lesbians armed with hog castrators and fly the Jolly Roger of bloody Kotex, nor succumb to the blandishments of a veteran queen in drag of Liz in riding pants. Even the Terrible Mother will be touched by the grace of process.

So leave us throw aside the drained crankcase of Brubeck and proceed to unleaven the yeast bread of cunt and unfurl the jolly condom. . . . I walk up to this chick, flash a condom on her like a piecea tin, you dig, and I say, "Come with me."

"Fresh," she say and slap me hard, the way I know it is this impersonator is a insult. I insinuate a clap up her ass without so much as by-your-leave.

So I says, "I thought you was McCoy. You look so nice and female to an old cowhand."

"Oh go impersonate a purple-assed baboon, you stupid old character. I'd resist you to the last bitch in any sex."

I stand on the Fifth Amendment, will not answer question of the senator from Wisconsin. "Are you or have you ever been a member of the male sex?" They can't make Dicky whimper on the boys. Know how I take care of crooners, don't you? Just listen to them. A word to the wise guy. I mean you gotta be careful of politics these days, some old department get physical kick him right in his Coordinator. Well, that's the hole story, and I guess I oughta know after all these years. Wellcome and Burroughs to the family party, a member in *hrumph* good standing we hope.

Castrates, Don't Let The Son Set On You Here—precocious little prick could get it by ass mosses. (Seaweed in a dark green grotto.)

The Philosophic Doctor sits on his rattan-ass Maugham veranda drinking pink gin fades to a Manhattan analyst looking over a stack of notes.

"So our murder was, it seems, the bitten Brubeck, who has since recovered and spread his hideous progeny from the wards of Seattle to the parishes of New Orleans, nameless blubby things crawl out of ash pits all covered with shitty sheets, walk around gibber like dead geese."

This refers to a nightmare of the subject's childhood in which he found himself threatened by two figures covered with soiled sheets—poison juices, Goddammit! Dream occur after the subject's collaborating father read him "The Murders in the Rue Morgue," where, as you will doubtless recall, one woman got her head cut clean off and rammed up the chimney. So, Brubeck, you know what you can do with your Liz bitch; and if you don't, my orangutan friend will show you.

"I have frequently observed in the course of my practices, *hrumph*, I mean practice, that homosexuals often express a willingness to, *humph*, copulate with *headless* women—a consummation devoutly to be wished. As one subject expressed it, 'Now I read where this chicken live a week without a head. They feed it through this tube stick out so the neck don't heal over and close up the way a cunt would heal over she didn't open it up every month with an apple corer, to let the old blood out. I mean a broad don't need that head anyhoo.' And recall that it was Medusa's head turned the boys to stone. I suggest that the perilous part of a woman is her hypothalamus, sending solid female static fuck up a man's synapses and leave him paralyzed from the waist down."

So I am prepared to state that the above is true and accurate to the best of my knowledge, so help me God or any other outfit when my dignity and sovereignty be threatened by brutal short-arm aggression. Sworn before me, Harry Q. T. Burford on this day.

"We must have a long talk, son. You see there are men and there are, well, women; and women are different from men."

"In precisely what way, Father?" said young Cesspoll incisively.

"Well, they're, well, they're different, that's all. You'll understand when you're older; and, *hurumph*, that's what I want to talk to you about. When you *do* get older."

"Come see me tonight in my apartment under the school privy.

Show you something interesting," said the janitor, drooling green coca juice.

Women seethe with hot poison juices eat it off in a twink. Laws of hospitality be fucked. Take your recalcitrant ass to your own trap. No drones in my dormitories.

"I'm no one's live one," sneered the corpse to the necrophile. "Go back to your own people, you frantic old character."

"Oh be careful. There they go again," says the old queen as his string break, spilling his balls across the floor. "Stop them, will you, James, you worthless old shit! Don't just stand there and let the master's balls roll into the coal bin."

"Is them my peeled balls those kids play marbles with? Why shit sure. Boy, who give you the right to play with my balls?"

"They revert to the public domain after not being claimed forty year, mister."

Well, the wind-up is the fag marries the transvestite Liz disguised as a boy in drag, former heartthrob of Greg hang him for kicks and retire to a locker in Grand Central, subsisting on suitcase and shoe leather. So many tasty ways to prepare it, girls—simmered in saddle soap, singe-broiled in brilliantine, smoked over smoldering ashtrays.

We are in a long white corridor of leaves lithp sunlight.

The Old West dies slow on Hungarian gallows, so while he is fixing (can't hit the hypothalamus anymore) we will shake down the trap for hidden miles and tragic flaws hang a golden lad with his own windblown hair.

When is a boy not a boy? When he is buoyed up by the wind, and the sailplane falls silent as erection.

The blind vet is on the way over to fuck me in the Grand Canal bent over the Academy Bridge. Someone take a picture and cops the film fest for a big brass bidet.

The lamprey seeks a silver fish in the green lagoon.

It would be better off dead. Broken leg. Told by an idiot broken down there you must hear. It is out of the woodpile and into the fire that monkey, and Denmark is rotten with a funeral pyre of bullshit.

"Look into my eyes, baby, mirror of the mad come."

"I can see inside the blue flames running on these long white nerves burn the spine in a slow squeeeeeeeeze."

Mouths leap forward on flesh tubes, clamp and twist.

Johnny on all fours and Marv sucking him and running his fingers down the thigh backs and light over the ass and outfields of the ball park. Johnny's body begins to hump in the middle, each hump a little longer and squeezier like oily fingers inside squeeze your balls soft as pink down, squeeze those sweet marshmallows slow slow slow.

He throws his head back with a great wolf howl.

Call the coroner; my skill naught avail.

Mine it out of your limestone bones, those fossil messages of arthritis; read the metastasis with blind fingers.

Where else you gonna look? Into the atrophied nuts of the priest, coyote of death? (A coyote is character hangs around the halls of the immigration department in Mexico, D.F., engage to help you for a fee with his inside connections.)

"I can get you straight in to the District Supervisor. Got an in. Of course, it cost. I don't want much—all go pay off my *tremendous* connections." His voice breaks in a pathic scream.

"Didja get a stand-on?" said the vulgar old queen to the virginal boy, trembling in white flame of contempt. "Land sakes," said the queen, "so young so cold so fair—I love it." (Silver statue in the moonlight.)

The swindler enters Heaven in a blast of bullshit. Here's a man hang self opening night of the Met. Cut throat of entire staff, take over the stage, single-handed scene-stealer. Prance out in Isolde drag, sing the "Liebestod" in a hideous falsetto, ending in burlesque striptease. "Take it off! Take it off!" chant his stooges, as pink step-ins, stiff with ass blood, fly out over the audience, she spring the trap. Blood burn to neon pink light through his spine spasms and grinding bone grins. Flesh turn to black shit and flake off—wind and rain and bones on mouldy beach. The queen is a hard-faced boy, patch over one eye, parrot on shoulder, say, "Dead men tell no tales—or do they?" He prods the skull with a cutlass, and a crab scuttles out. The boy reaches down and pick up a scroll.

"The Map! The Map!"

The map turns to shitty toilet paper in his hands, blow across a vacant lot in East St. Louis, catch on clean barbed wire and burn with a blue flame.

The boy pulls off the patch, parrot flies into the jungle, cutlass turns to machete. He is studying the Map and swatting sand flies.

The author has gathered his multiple personalities for a rally at Tent City on the banks of the river Jordan. "Come on in and park your piles, boys. You is Burroughs and Wellcome. Now I wanta hear something artistic like the time you got out of that old black Model A, Cowper's juice seeping right through your thin schoolboy slacks, and jack off into the dogwood and your jissom turn to little white flowers in the air fall so slow and sweet through the air.

"He's the Last Dead End Kid."

"He ain't talking."

"Well, let him soften up a bit."

"Wait till his balls dissolve down to little black frog eggs." (Tadpoles wriggle away in the black lagoon.) "Then he'll talk, and be glad to talk."

"Yonny, glo home."

"This *is* my home, you Chinaman cocksucker. Fuck off, you! And remember, there is only one captain of those shits—as I affectionately call my S.P.s, Subsidiary Personalities. You nothing but an L.S.P.: *Local* Subsidiary Personality. Get forward, or I shall put a ball through all your heads."

"You don't got the balls, Gertie."

"Why, you Southern white trash rim a shittin' nigger for an eyecup of P.G.!"

"You dare get sassy and fat with me? You tired old Southern belle, nobody care if you come in or not except for your unsanitary habits eatin' with prehensile piles the way it break up the Family Reunion."

"And what's eatin' you, you little intimidate prick? Nobody goin' to cut our nuts off while I'm around, and I can kick the shit out of any Liz inna Zone. Now we drop that fucking *Lucha Libre* dyke down the marl hole she crawl up out of. Strictly from Loch Ness. Strange and undesirable serpent. So for the Chrissake, kid—make with the smile. The show must go on.

"And as for you, you black-assed mealy-mouthed cuntsucker always mutter around about, 'Lawsy, boss, I believe in life, boss,' just as sure as that old river yonder, life flow through you, sit still in the springtime, wash me back to old Virginia and cornhole me up my tater . . . spitting cotton."

A delicious *frisson* offer up your pink ass sweat like a young boy's lip to a black buck in a nigger shack make you scream and whisper and moan for it. "Aw now I couldn't screw the young Massa! I'm a *good* nigger."

"I'll teach you to brown a golden lad, you hog-balled bastard. Come hawg-cutting day. Hmm, on second thought . . ."

"Please! Rasmus, please!"

"I ain't uppity, boss. Better put your pants on. Might dirty your little white ass sitting around naked in a nigger shack."

"Yes, sir, that old river seen a heap of folks come and go, shit and die. He flood out in the spring, and he shrink down in the long heat of summer, them crawdads crawl way down into the earth. Ever suck the sweet cool water up out of a crawdad hole?"

"For the love of God, sheriff, lock up this rusty word hoard."

"Now, you nameless assholes, remember I do the shitting around here, *all* the shitting; and any wise prick try to dip into my ass is going to be kicked right down the marl hole with the Gibbering Larvals. I mean, show your culture. When the Massa shits, keep your distance, folks. He is subject to eject a choking cloud of dried yellow hepatitis fallout." (A puffball bursts in Missouri field. Dry heat of August. Sound of insects.)

"Now it is chiefly you two half-assed entities I am concerned with. Your recalcitrant and perfidious maneuvers constitute a menace to the enterprise, which, as I well aware, you sworn to sabotage. Scumunist pricks, slop out of my public trough. And the Chink Dummy yacks party line on a queer barstool, blatting out the Formulas of Doom. And you, Johnny-Come-Lately, advance and be recognized. What're you now, a cock biter? Well, I don't think we have an opening for a man of your caliber. Keep you on file."

"Filthy little beast." She tweaks the Child in the nuts, and he doubles over retching. "Faugh!" she screams, starting back. "Bitch dog! Puking cock-roach!" She splits his lips with an expert one-finger slap—like a dog chain across the face.

He looks at her face gray as junk eyes betrayed to death go out in empty light sockets. Blue smoke drifts out.

Come in, please! Come in, please! Can't move a cell of my body without got the Word. I'm a synopsis Latah. Nobody know my trouble, and especially not Jesus, the miracle artist. Something he don't like? Go make with the miracle, James, I show you how. Now the perpetrating of miracles constitute a brazen attempt to louse up the universe. When you set up something as MIRACLE, you deny the very concept of FACT, establish a shadowy and spurious court infested by every variety of coyote and shady fixer, *beyond* Court of Fact.

Idiot raconteur cling to you like a linguaphone. Ever hear "This is the penwiper of my brother-in-law" repeat a million times? Once those sockets in your head, can't turn nobody out no more. The sockets weep little tears of blue flame.

Now look, none of this trying to slide in the pitch on the chick deal you got cooking. Back there in Bebop jive talk. This is not an escort service but a functioning (after a fashion) organism. Positively no pimping in the aorta.

Run fingers over her chassis light as moths leave little blue phosphorescent wake burn slow behind. Converge a soft blue crackle up her cunt and burn inside her begin to squirm and wiggle and moan. (Burn her tits.)

"Of *course* I'm sure of ultimate 'victory,' but the little prick's got the orgone supply sew tight up as young boy nuts."

"We gotta find a way to get at it, boss."

"Mindless idiot! The only way to get at it is through him."

"Well, we gotta con him."

"How do you mean? Like this? 'Of course you know I'm down here from Front Office, con you back into a Gibbering Larval and take over the orgone supply. Now this con involves Duty, HIGHER DUTY and *32nd DEGREE DUTY*, all of which devolve on you should act precise like I prefer it.' "

They'll move in right away, take a girl over, piss out her cock and start farting code to the Enemy. "It's a fifth column, is what it is," I said to Luke only yesterday. "We should pass it along to the Torso, come down from Cleveland take care of those pricks."

"Smartest thing is not to let me in first base. Once I get my little foot through that door, which you would be well advised not to open—I mean a con like that require personality. . . . Wouldn't you?"

"Well, we gotta talk to him straight, man to man: 'Now, kid, *you* want something, *I* want something. I do something for you, you do something for me. That's the way the ball bounces."

The Child blasts all his teeth out in a great Bronx cheer. (Pansy dressed in spring robes catch them in butterfly net, throw them at the boy's mouth; they float back and fit into a whitewashed brick wall.)

They was ripe for the plucking, forgot way back yonder in that cornhole, lost in little scraps of delight and burning scrolls.

The Egyptian struts in with hump of racial hate on his back, feeds off him regular as clockwork—big fat boy in there swill butter and animal fats in the worst form there is.

(Oh, death, where is thy sting? The Man is never on time.) Corseted Tenor: "You and I are good for nothing but pie." Steak and kidney pie is served in top hats by naked chorus girls—pubic hairs, finger toe nails and teeth silver painted.

Crystal oaks and pines and persimmons light up green and purple and blue and deep cherry red, frozen in pathic postures. Heavy snow opportunely blankets arrival of W.Q. "Fats" Terminal, cosmic horse's ass.

I am looking over a river in Tolima—section of Colombia where is much leprosy and guerrilla war—through cardboard opera glasses of leprosy.

"How did you get this terrible habit, kid?"

"In the family. The Garcías have always been lepers, and proud of it. You bet I'm going back to Carville."

"Put a Direction Finder on the Chink, smell out that Controller."

The Private Eye strips to bulletproof plastic transparent magnifying shorts.

"Show you something interesting." He switches on his pelvis. "Light all the veins in my prick. Beautiful pink sight."

The plague break out in the lobby of the U.N. Victims are spirited away in black Cadillacs, flushed down a garbage disposal unit in a special kitchen of the Arab delegates where a man knew what to do with his fat old dog offend with halitosis. Sidi Slimano turn up the garbage disposal full blast, shake the house like a tornado—he leap onto the kitchen table, do a Russian dance with shrill "hy, hy, hy"s and a Negro janitor, with a eunuch jockstrap over his balls, feed the yipping dog into the unit, hair and blood spurt out 1963 on the wall.

"Yes sir, boys, the shit really hit the fan in '63," said the tiresome old prophet can bore the shit out of you in any space-time direction. "Now I happen to remember because it was just two years before that a strain of human aftosa developed in a Bolivian laboratory got loose through the medium of a chinchilla coat fix an income tax case in Kansas City. When it hit New York and everybody with long streamers hang out the mouth, the town look like one big toffee pull. The Abolitionists hanged a purple-assed baboon in Buckingham Palace, and 'Fats' Terminal, dressed in his Home Secretary suit, sucked it off *in extremis*. Cutaway pants, rubber prick two feet long sticking out, ejaculated Black Widows all over the palace. (The Queen is still shit-scared of the W.C.)

"Now it was just one month before that I was took bad with the menstrual cramps. And a Liz claimed immaculate conception give birth to a six-ounce Spider Monkey thooh the navel—they say the croaker was party to that caper had the monkey on his back all the time. 1963 a dream meet with a Mexican bank robbery."

The Arab plays a flute, and the unit undulates up out of the sink on a long flexible metal tube. It gives a great Bronx cheer, and the Arab delegates scream away in burning Cadillacs.

A Negro boy in turtleneck red sweater dances fearless with the unit under the flickering white light of a Coleman gasoline lamp in an East Texas barn.

"Undulate me, baby; and let me undulate you." The unit nips him playfully on the ear, and a drop of blood falls onto his sweater.

Under icebergs and fjords where naked nymphs goose each other with classic pictures, sooner or later knock a girl up with a tintype, her give birth to a penny arcade.

"I'm a slow man with a mustache," said the colonel know how to give a girl the time.

"Land's sake, like a hundred little scrub women with pink down brushes scrub your cunt out with ambergris it turn to a conch and give a weird Attic wail." (Fade out. Jungle calls. The kid stirs muttering in malarial sleep, and Pan pipes drift down the Andes.)

Death comes slow on Hungarian gallows. "When you gonna pull my leg, get this show on the road?" he gags, his face tumescent with lust.

"Daddy, that old nigger shit sure do Number Two right on my tummy-wummy."

"What's that you say, girl? That black bastard. A judgment on me for eatin' the coon pone. A man's sins do trail him like a fart into Mrs. Worldly's drawing room, stamp him REJECT." (The butler puts the Blue Seal on his haunch, while Mrs. Kindheart politely blinds herself with Sani-flush.)

"Don't you fret, sweet thing. Me and the boys take care of that nigger when Hawg Day rolls around."

The *diseuse*, in hillbilly dress with a necklace of hog castrators tinkling in the pink dawn, passes a ruined outhouse (Piney Woods backdrop), sings "When Hawg Day rolls around." The sunrise catches an armadillo rooting in a weed-grown field.

"Girl, it's time you learn where castrates come from . . . blub blub."

"Yes poppa eat it lovely old moleskin way."

"Let me be your mole cricket, lady." Candy tongue melt up in there, light up your pink coral grotto.

Nineteen-ten whorehouse: black silk stocking, white skin: black pubic hair, black-and-white photos. A huge Victrola plays slow and mournful through a vast horn to howling whores. (Drunk, with a top hat and a mustache, takes off his hat and gives a reverent Bronx cheer.)

Satyr runs down a garden path, marine shoots pink ping-pong balls from tommy gun, rain off his ass turn to little red candy pillows. Armadillos gambol up and eat them in the satyr's wake.

"I want you to *smell* this barstool," said the paranoid ex-Communist to the manic FBI agent. "Stink juice—and you may quote me—has been applied by paid hoodlums constipated with Moscow *goldwasser*." (The water cure, comrade. So I should take the active part in this horrible synopsis?)

Dirty snow melt in the spring hatch these frozen niggers out the woodpile.

Some cowboy ride around with the noose on, looking for his last roundup.

"I live with my boots off," The Singing Tumbleweed told your reporter, leaning against the whitewashed brick wall of heroin slowdown.

"I'll cut your white pecker throat and leave you a squaaawwking chicken. I'm nobody's fool—good public school of hard knockers and know how to handle this horrible case. When is a woman not a woman? When I cut her motherfucking head off."

(Note: When your reporter was learning to be a pilot, this young angel of a cadet dive on this old gash in a field. Her run instead of flop when he buzz her, he cut her head off with his wings. The commandant's press agent referred to "this horrible case.")

So I am in Mrs. Bridey Murphy's chowder along with the overalls. The Interrogator operate on the boys and the girls and the cats and the rats, leave them grope for lost balls through a maze of movies and burlesques and penny arcades. (Mad-eyed jungle rats die with a Gallic shrug—"*Zut alors! Quoi faire?*")

"What are you doing?" said the torso artist to his colleague.

"Just experimenting. Interesting relation between pain, fear and

the *harumph* doctor—and nothing more interesting than this phe-
nomenon." He shows his hard prick. "Now touch it just there.
. . . See how it pulses. And now I am going to conceive The Great
Work," he says, shitting on the laboratory floor. "I have created
life!!" he screams, pointing to a roundworm undulating up out of
the shit, give a Bronx cheer, grow to a great serpent with lamprey
mouth and chase the "scientist" through his Yokohama appliances.

"There are some things of which I cannot even bring myself to
squeak," said the rat. "The things a girl sees in a warehouse!"

Cute little agent use sex as a weapon, crucify an old queen with
neon nails, run up the black wind sock over burning boys in a
plane crash (all those innocent young male screams). The old queen
breathe in the Black Snake. "That hits so good." (Young male
screams drift in on the warm spring wind, stir boy hair in the carny
night stand so sweet so cold so fair popping pink gum bubbles,
look into the penny arcade, petals of young sweat caught in the
lip down make your mouth water for stuff.)

"Cardinal, can you stand up there in the very ass of God which
you have plugged with the Pope, that veteran horse's ass and cosmic
brown-nose?"

Will the gentle reader get up off his limestone and pick up the
phone?

Cause of death: completely uninteresting.

The Voices rush in like burning lions.

"I'll rip through you," said, trembling, the Man of Black Bones.

"So told Lieutenant LeBee, whose auntie was drowned at sea,"
said a little squeegee voice.

"Cross crystal pains of horror to the tilted pond."

"Time to retire. . . . Get a frisk . . . glittering worms of nostalgia's
call house where young lust flares over the hills of home, and
jissom floats like cobwebs in a cold spring wind."

"Lovely brown leg. Oh Lordy me baby on the brass bed, and bedbugs crawl under the blue light. . . . Oh God."

"All the day you do it. . . . Do it right now."

"Suck the night tit under the blue flame of Sterno. . . . Orient pearls to the way they should go. . . ."

"The winged horse and the mosaic of iron cut the sky to blue cake. . . ."

"On crystal balconies pensive angels study pink fingernails. Gilt flakes fall through the sunlight."

"Distant rumble of stomachs. Porcine fairies wave thick wallets. Bougainvillea covers the limestone steps. Poisoned pigeons rain from the Northern Lights, plop with burning wings into dry canals. The Reservoirs are empty. Blue stairs end, spiral down, suffocate . . . where brass statues crash through the hungry squares and alleys of the gaping city. . . ."

"Iridescent hard-on . . . Rainbow in the falls."

"Can't hear nothing."

"Two kids got relief."

"Never more the goose honks train whistle bunkmate. . . . Man in Lower Ten (eyes caked with mucus) watch the boy get a hard-on."

"Not a mark on him. What killed his monkey?"

"Suicide God, take the back-street junk route. Detours of the fairy canyon shine in the light of dawn. Buildings fall through dust to the plain of salt marshes. Are the boys over the last ridge and into the safe harbor of Cunt Lick, where no wind is?"

"By the squared circle, cut cock, my mouth, the cunt of and the rag on. Bring your own wife. . . . Panama Flo, the sex fiend, beat the Gray Nurse for steak-sized chunks." (The Gray Nurse is most dangerous form of shark. Like all sharks they bite out steak-sized chunks.)

"Wouldn't you?"

"Libido is dammed by the Eager Beaver."

"Notice is served on toilet paper."

"Smell shock grabs the lungs with nausea."

Fat queen, bursting out of dungarees, carry a string of bullheads to the tilted pond.

"TILT."

Gray head bob up in the old swimming hole. The boys climb up each other, scream, "EEEEK! A man!"

"He will be fetched down, this creature."

"A fairy."

"Monstrous!"

"Fantastic!"

"Get her!"

"Slam the steel shutter of latency!"

"Radius radius. It is enough."

"Doctorhood is being made with me."

Middle-aged Swede in yachting cap, naked tattooed torso, neutral blue eyes, gives a shot of heroin to the schizophrenic (whiff of institution kitchens). Gray ghosts of a million junkies bend close as the Substance drains into living flesh.

"Is this the fix that staunched a thousand shits and burnt the scented drugstores of Lebanon?"

Student in medieval hose and doublet with cock guard: "If a cat hath nine lives, verily this olde pricke of mine hath nine childhoods, each more maudlin than its fellow."

The professor is caught short and shits in a piece of newspaper, rolls it up and throws it at a passing citizen of indeterminate nationality who screams curses in twenty languages living and dead.

"It's a cheap Shanty Irish trick, shitting in a piece of paper and throwing it at passersby."

"So who's lace-curtain? This stark young novelist like a dirty windswept street." Fade out 1920s tunes, fireworks cover stutter of machine-gun fire from black Cadillacs longer and lower, fade into Soviet tanks.

"One of my earliest memories was a bull's-eye score scored by Mary O'Toole the local Liz on a dignified old junky so loaded he didn't register. Just walk along with shit dripping off his pan, a boyish smile on his lips. I shall never forget that smile . . . in times of affliction such as come to any woman. Goddammit, another impersonator! Be there a man with soul so dead to himself have never said this is my own my native ass?"

American queens shriek and howl in revolting paroxysms of self-pity. They declare a nausea contest. The most abject queen of them all gathers his rotting protoplasms for an all-out effort. . . .

"My power's coming! . . . My power's coming!" he screeches.

Orchestra strikes up, and female impersonator prances out in hillbilly drag with hairy knobby knees showing.

"She'll be swishing round the mountain when she comes. . . ."

The queen's familiar spirits are gathering, larval whimpering entities. The queen writhes in a dozen embraces, accommodating the passionate exigencies of invisible partners, now sucking noisily, now throwing his legs over his head with a loud "Whoopeee!" He sidles across the floor with his legs spread, reaches up and caresses one of the judges with a claw . . . he has turned himself into a monster crab with a human body from the waist down. Beneath the skin liquid protoplasm quivers like jellied consommé as he offers up his ass.

The judges start back, appalled.

"He liquefy himself already!"

"Deplorable!"

Other contestants jealously throw off their clothes to reveal an impressive variety of unattractive physiques.

"Look at me!"

"Feast your eyes on *my* ugliness!"

One queen pulls the falsie top off his pinhead and begins cackling like a chicken: "I don't need that old head anyhoo!"

Junky furnished room opens on red-brick slum—young addict, sculpted to bone and muscle, probes for a blue vein with a brass needle in his smooth white arm.

Mexican finca: drunken machos in dark glasses reel about on the patio, blasting at terrified cats with .45 automatics. All wear two-hundred-dollar English suits and drink Old Pharr Scotch from bottles. They miss the cats, wound each other, scream "*¡Chinga!*" in chorus as each empties his gun into a compañero.

Barefoot, ragged boys steal in, silent as dawn. Hideous atomic mutations, some miss a lower jaw, others have two black holes and no nose. They strip the bodies, drink the Scotch—one born without a mouth sticks a bottle up his ass and tilts his body forward. They put on the suits, which hang on them in folds, and posture in parody of drunken machos, spitting, patting .45s, flashing police badges and nude pictures of Chapultepec blonds. Exit boys without a sound.

Sunrise. Vultures settle, peck at dark glasses.

Modern apartment *a là swish*. Fags and old women gabble and giggle faster and faster, scream past each other at supersonic speed.

Blue-walled Arab whorehouse. Outside, the yipes of rioters; shop shutters slam, Arab music blasts from loudspeakers mixed with Radio Cairo like a berserk tobacco auction. Fades to flutes of Ramadan.

—

Stop! Here is Terminal!

W.Q. "Fats" Terminal wake with a fart and let out a bray can be heard for blocks.

"I have arisen, Goddammit! Fetch the royal lounging robes!"

His secretary trots in, a huge slovenly man in filthy sweatshirt and rusty black pants. "Fats" struggles into his purple bathrobe and straps on his cavalry sword, with which he decapitated the Countess de Perrier's Russian wolfhound. A long-ago garden party in his slim youth, before he was blacklisted by every embassy and hostess in the world.

He barely escaped with his life from Seville after a perfect kill, and the noble bull dying and the matador talk to it soft and nasty sweet and everybody silent, "Fats" loose his terrible Bronx cheer, leap down into the arena and kick the dying bull in the nuts.

"Fats" is connected in some unspecified way with every underground of the world: Mafia, IRA, Bolivian Trotskyites, PDL, EOKA, Islam, Inc., Arab Brotherhood, Mau Mau. He expresses himself typically on all movements and leaders of movements: "Black-assed cocksuckers don't know their piles from a finger stall. They couldn't resist a virus. What I think about Sidi?" He lets out his famous Bronx cheer.

No resistance movement dares to dispense with his "services." He edits a newspaper known as the *Underground Express*, mostly consists of bulletins and trade gossip: "What well-known asshole currently throbs to a DARK HORSE? Is my cunt red? All Mau Mau requested to castrate themselves if captured, to foil the degenerate appetites of English Capitalist hangman Smithers 'The Nance' Macintosh, who was drummed out of the Black Watch for importuning the Crown Prince with prehensile piles at the Queen's funeral."

"I think Fats is swell," said the inspirational female analyst.

"A preposterous slander!" shrieks Dr. Burger.

"We are at a loss," snarls Brundage the Insolvent, dissolving in a pool of shit.

"Clearly an anal type," observes Dr. Burger severely. "Faugh!"

"Discrimination!" screams a Negro fag, high on injustice.

"So I hung an albatross. . . . It was my training done it, born and bred to hang dat cocksucker."

"We hear it was the other way around, Doc," said the snide reporter with narrow shoulders and bad teeth.

The doctor's face crimsons. "And I wish to state that I have been doctor at Dankmoor Prison thirty years man boy and bestial and I always keep my nose clean . . . never compromise myself to be alone with the hanged man, always insist on presence of my baboon assistant, witness and staunch friend in any position."

"Oral breakthrough," lisped the skeleton.

"Very likely," said the Horse Trader, spitting out all his teeth.

"Orgone service is terrible around here," said the rectal cancer case.

"Already loth my ath inna thervith," lisped out the hole in his side.

"God purge me of the black yen for his bones," whimpered the aging queen, her prick dropping like a wind sock where there is no wind.

Negroes thin and brittle as smooth black sticks cut each other with sneering razors. No surrender in yellow eyes like incandescent gold.

Adolescent hoodlums have crucified Christ with Bronx cheers, go honkytonking and nobody give a shit when He give up the Ghost.

And "Fats" bites into a sandwich. "Butter!" he screams. "They is trying to poison me with cholesterol!"

—

The young rustler is apprehended by his friend at the old swimming hole. Under the eyes of giggling boys he is hanged from the diving branch, pirouettes in the air with an *entrechat* six—breathless pause at leap top.

"Let this be a lesson to you boys," said the old sheriff, eyes pale and empty as blue sky over the neon midways of America.

Shattering bloody blue of Mexico, brains spilled in the cocktail lounge, white leather and blue silk, and the fat macho substance in dark glasses has burned down the jai alai bookie with his obsidian-handled forty-five.

Heart in the sun, headless snake, hanged man's cock pulsing on the holy gallows, pantless corpses hang from posts along the road to Monterrey.

The boys whistle and wolf-call. One catches jissom in a straw hat and passes it around in obscene, begging pantomime and each boy jacks off into it. A boy twangs the rope and sings like an angel, voice clear, hard, metallic as wind in high wires over a gorge, waterfalls and rainbow.

"Watch those prehensile tensions!" screams the belching Technician . . . as the bridge wires snap, spill screaming hot rods into the void.

"Play chicken with gravity, you little pricks!" snarls the Technician. "I told them the fucking bridge wasn't worth a—" He farts loud and ugly.

The great black crab penetrated with air-pistol pellet oozes watery crankcase oil.

The rope rot through, the rustler falls white as Narcissus into the black water, glides down. The boys lean over to watch the descent of the god, dissolve in sunlight, see hairs sharp as fine wire and teeth and freckles—their mourning selves. The sheriff is muttering through his toothless mean old-woman mouth, "Now, I want you fellows to wear trunks. . . . Decent women with telescopes can see you. We've had complaints."

The boy floats white as marble in the swimming hole, with a lamprey at his side where Christ's blood flowed and the colostomy came out spurting shit.

"Let me do a suck job on you," said the old queen with a lamprey mouth. A great silver fish goes over the falls with a lamprey on its side, into the rainbow.

Pinks and blues of 1920s tune drift into the locker room and the two boys, first time tea-high, jack off to "My Blue Heaven." What are we going to do with all the golden lads? Not enough train whistles and fights against the house odds. "I just can't get you a fight, kid. Things are tough."

Police bullet in the alley, broken wings of Icarus and screams of a burning boy inhaled by the old junky, eyes empty as a vast plain—husk of vulture wings in dry air—pulls the pale smoke into his screaming lungs and his body squirms in the Black Massage.

They walk down Lindell and into the house surrounded by deserted factories and junkyards; weeds and vines and the sound of insects. They undress slow in a mirror-lined room, fuck all the way out and back across backyards, ash pits and bars, stickball games, virginal lots (little green snakes under rusty iron), cats copulate and boys jack off in packing crate.

The pusher dropped around to leave his card. "Like the song say, 'I'll be around.' " Looking for a vein with a tattoo needle, the boy's chest is marked over the hard limestone bone with blue bites.

The wind shakes billowing brass like yellow silk.

Lick of junk sickness eats at your heels like a dream rat, gnaw the shiny white tendons probing for a vein of iron.

Chorus of Midwest fairies sing "Glow Worm" with lighted wands . . . plaintive purple ghosts in the June night.

" 'Tain't human. Devil doll . . ." The Controller hides in some ultimate privy on a black windy slope of the Andes under a sky green as neon.

Great fat queen in a huge baby carriage pushed by a brutal-faced, gum-chewing Italian with long sideburns and a white silk vest. "AWWWWWW!" squalls the queen. And the Italian changes her diapers absently, his eyes follow a woman's haunches down the street and into the butcher shop.

Masochist queen refuse to leave burning warehouse because her hand-trucking lover won't carry him.

Empty waxen child faces, the teeth go first.

Over the hills to the lonesome pines of Idaho, where boy hearts pulse on Christmas trees, and ski-jumpers whistle over our heads like bullets in the crystal night . . .

The boy is pure sad, all hate faded like smoke in the dawn wind, clear and calm sad forever.

Carnival of splintered pink peppermint. Black mustache and child screams after his lost balloon like a frustrated cocksucker. Tattooed sailor leaves the penny arcade with firm young ass.

"Oh, those Golden Slippers—" Copper-luster chamber pots, brass spittoons, black smoke on the hip in the Chink laundry.

Ski run revisited by old queen, his friend killed there in 1928, black and empty against the vacationing sky.

"You're nothing but a larval," sneered one subsidiary personality to another. "I'm a decent entity at least, got some outlines to me."

So this is the Burroughs special, a dash and a soupçon, a pinch and a handful. If you all like it not, will distribute to the school privy of the world for a glorious burial. Young asses wiped all over the world, white ass and black ass, yaller ass and copper ass, pink ass and bronze ass.

Two gentlemen opponents square off on the country club lawn. With a bestial snarl one throws up his knee with murderous force. The other pivots deftly, jabbing for his opponent's eyes with forked fingers. They roll in the grass, screaming like mandrills and clawing at each other's eyes and genitals.

Old Colonel nudges Sir Granville Heatherstone: "This is tasty."

Sanitarium grounds 1917—junkies sit under spreading oaks in the Indian summer of Iowa. Nurses bustle along with busy hypos.

"Now, Mr. Harmon, you know you only get five grains."

"Oh I think you're terrible, Mr. Hardwith."

They sprawl in green chairs, faces dead as the garroted. "And where the dead leaf fell, there it did rest."

Peacocks scream in the red crystal dawn. Golden apple of woman breast swells bronze souvenir ashtray. He sits up and looks into a cobra lamp.

On a white alabaster bed a Negress black as opium does slow bumps and grinds. "Haven't got a thing to say," he sneered through his plastic surgeon nose.

The gray-faced queen with dark glasses and purple lips sneers and shoves it in gear and shoots away . . . a white-faced boy carries a dead dog from the suburb road.

Cursed down your years with a yen like an open needle sore, coal and junk, cancer and black oil in the blood and bones. Ink in the white bones. Black blood from the ruptured crab.

Porpoises with pink ribbon nooses around their necks pilot the ship to anchor at vast Venetian mooring posts in an endless oily rubbish heap. The ship is stuck in black slime and garbage and rusty iron. The porpoises fade with a Bronx cheer and a distant boat whistle. . . .

"I am the Egyptian," he said, looking all flat and silly.

And I said, "Really, Bradford, don't be tiresome."

Old dank garden in the Midwest August moon, pool full of leaves in black iridescent water.

Would it be forgiven the rising young diplomat occasional slip and shit on the floor by the punch bowl? Or absently offer his prick instead of his hand to Nikki from the Russian Embassy? Or now and then leap up like the savant in reverse, as though catapult by unseen hand, and fart loud and ugly in Mrs. Worldly's face?

Could grace or charm give these faults a snow job, sure Reggie has them all.

Insouciance of a child awakened from sleep with a sulky hard-on in the green summer dawn, boy-grin on sunlit water. Hot rod piloted by a debased and brutal angel screams through pregnant Indian women, leave all behind a wake of blood and afterbirths, throw out a blast of condoms with Bronx cheer.

"Just see me, a fourteen-year-old boy," said the skinny old queen. "I've never been fucked before so I wander down into Mexican town and this copper youth in white pants call me over, make sullen and bestial motions—I bend over and drop my pants. He fucks me with furious quivering contempt that melts my whole pelvis down onto his cock like a glob of gold."

Death rows the boy like sleeping marble down the Grand Canal in a gondola of gold and crystal . . . poles out into a vast lagoon: souvenir postcards and bronzed baby shoes, Grand Canyon and Niagara Falls, Chimborazo, New York skyline and Aztec pyramid. Pinks and blues and yellows of religious objects in the Catholic store on a red-brick square surrounded by trees.

"All right. You're paying for it," said the Mexican.

"Only fools do those villains pity who are punished ere they have done their mischief," said the young Billy Budd as he innocently cut the throats of his lifeboat mates. "Such a thing as too much fun," he adds primly. "Besides which they was eatin' me out of house and home. Nip it in the bud, Mary, nip it in the bud."

Frenzied dinosaurs uncover a fossil man. . . .

In the attic of the Big Store on bolts of cloth we made it, careful don't spill, don't rat on the boys. Light cuts through the dark chasm, dust in sunlight, the cellar is full of light and air . . . in two weeks the tadpoles hatch. I wonder what ever happened to Otto's boy who played the violin?

—

Pages blew out across the winds and rubbish of Mexico. . . .
A boy squats by a mud wall whistling mambo through his teeth,
wipes his ass with a sheaf of manuscripts. Wind and rubble, vultures peck at fish heads. The boy stands up, shies a stone at the
vulture, vaults the wall and whistles away under dusty poplar trees
shake in the afternoon wind.

Spilt is the wastings of the cup. . . . "Take it away," he said
irritably.

The city mutters in the distance, pestilent breath of the cancerous librarian faint and intermittent in the warm spring wind.

Ruined porticoes and arabesques, boys playing languidly on the
vine-covered pyramids. Greg screws Brad on all fours, freeze into
a dirty picture in the withered hand of a very old queen.

"Is this a sex hang-up, Brad?" said the Chinese narcotic fuzz.

The decent women of America object. "Stay where you are!"
said Lithping Lu the Deputy. "You fruit varmints give me Burger's
disease in the worst form there is."

"I wouldn't put it in precisely those words," said Dr. Burger.

The man in a green suit—old-style English cut, with two side
vents and change pockets outside—will swindle the aging pro-
prietress of the florist shop. "Old flub gotta yen on for me."

The Grand Dragoness has given the order to her agents yack on
all the queer barstools in the world: "Get Burroughs." She gives
a little bump and fart. "It would be well not to fail."

"Continual assault of hostility," said the languid lavatory attendant. "Can't help it."

In a limestone gorge near East St. Louis, Illinois, met a copper
lad with a rusty loincloth crumble from his stiffening member seize
me in stone hands and fuck me with a crystal cock.

Interrupted by Paco, a little Spanish whore. Great pests from
little assholes grow. "Untimely comes this dirt," shrieked the poet
swallow forever the Perfect Line. What a con that was. . . . The

cast-off lover trailing broken potentials looks at me with reproach he can never formulate, sad and hostile sick conning eyes, feels with idiot slyness for the horrified cock.

"This is trivial," he said cunningly to the mastiff bitch.

"Satori," said the Zen monk. "I see . . ." He crosses the room and opens the door. "The Mons Calpa from Gibraltar."

—unload her unhatched shits upon us. "Another consignment of undesirables," sighed Immigration. "No, we do *not* admit advanced cases of lymphogranuloma, and we have no form of dole for disabled stool pigeon lost his voice in the service."

We are not at all innarested to find a prick crawl up the back stairs, make time in the broom closet, remember? and spurt all over the white sheet in the hung-over Sunday dawn. . . . We goin' to home it over the silver plate into the golden toilet and jack out our balls on the mosaic floor into the carp pool, keeps them healthy, fat and sluggish.

Assassin of geraniums! Murderer of the lilies!

Over the bridge to Brighton Rock, place of terrible pleasures and danger, where predatory brainwashers stalk the passersby in black Daimlers. Clients check Molotov cocktails and flamethrowers with the beautiful diseased hatcheck person of indeterminate sex. . . . And the government falls at least once a day.

Set wades in blood up to her cunt, cuts down the blasphemers of Ra with her sick hell of junk.

The snake's venom is paid for with coins of the realm of night. No hiding place . . .

Wooden steps wind up a vast slope, scattered stone huts. Greg licks the black rim of the world in a cave of rusty limestone. Across the hills to Idaho, under the pine trees, boys hang a horse with a broken leg. One plays "I'm Leavin' Cheyenne" on his harmonica, they pass around an onion and cry. They stand up and swing off through the branches with Tarzan cries.

We is all out on a long silver bail.

It was a day like any other when I walk down the Main Line to the Sargasso, pass faces set a thousand years in matrix of evil, faces with eerie innocence of old people, faces vacant of intent. Sit down in the green chair provided for me by other men occupy all the others. Convey my order with usual repetitions—at one time I was threatened by rum and Cinzano, whereas I order mint tea. I sit back and make this scene, mosaic of juxtapositions, strange golden chains of Negro substance seeped up from the Unborn South. So I do not at once dig the deformed child—I call it that for want of a better name: actually it look between unsuccessful baboon and bloated lemur, with a sort of moldy sour bestial look in the eyes—that was sitting to all intents and purposes on the back of my chair.

Shellac red-brick houses, black doors shine like ice in the winter sun. Lawn down to the lake, old people sit in green chairs, huddle in lap robes.

We are on the way over with a bolt of hot steel wool to limn your toilet with spangled orgones. Conspicuous consumption is rampant in the porticoes slippery with Koch spit, bloody smears on the cryptic mosaic—frozen cream cone and a broken dropper. As when a junky long dead woke with a junk-sick hard-on, hears the radiator thump and bellow like an anxious dinosaur of herbivorous tendencies—treeless plain stretch to the sky, vultures have miss the Big Meat. . . .

Will he fight? is the question at issue.

"Yes," snarls President Ra look up from a crab hunt, charge the Jockey Club with his terrible member. "Fuck my sewage canal, will you? Don't like you and don't know you. Some Coptic cock-sucker vitiate the pure morning joy of hieroglyph."

"At least we have saved the bread knife," he said.

"The message is not clear," said Garcia, when they brought him the *brujo* rapt in nutmeg.

Priest whips a yipping Sellubi down the limestone stairs with a gold chain.

"Unlawful flight to prevent consummation," lisps the toothless bailiff. The trembling defendant—survivor of the Coconut Grove fire—stands with a naked hard-on.

"Death by Fire in Truck," farts the Judge in code.

"Appeal is meaningless in the present state of our knowledge," says the defense, looking up from electron microscope.

"You have your warning," says the President.

"The monkey is not dead but sleepeth," brays Harry the Horse, with inflexible authority.

The centipede nuzzles the iron door rusted to thin black paper with urine of a million fairies. Red centipede in the green weeds and broken stelae. Inside the cell crouch prisoners of the Colónia. Mugwump sits naked on a rusty bidet, turns a crystal cylinder etched with cuneiforms. Iron panel falls in dust, red specks in the sunlight.

A vast Moslem muttering rises from the stone square where brass statues suffocate.